I Will Find the Answer

A Novel of Sherlock Holmes

By Kate Workman

Paperback ISBN 978-1-78092-015-3
ePub ISBN 978-1-78092-016-0
PDF ISBN 978-1-78092-017-7

Published in the UK by MX Publishing
335 Princess Park Manor, Royal Drive, London, N11 3GX
www.mxpublishing.com

Cover artwork by www.staunch.com

This novel is dedicated to, c
Doyle and Robert Louis Ste'
these characters and gave them to the
to acknowledge the masterful musicians, songwriters, and
singers who put together the musical *Jekyll and Hyde,*
especially for the songs *This is the Moment* and *In His
Eyes,* which initially got me addicted to the soundtrack
when I listened to them again back in 2008.

In addition, I'd like to dedicate this novel to Andrew
Shainberg, who didn't want me to write a particular short
story for a class, so instead I wrote the short story that
soon blossomed into this novel.

I also have to thank Edward Schwind, who gave me the
highest compliment a writer can ever receive--a non-
reader looking forward everyday to reading the next
handwritten segment I'd gotten done. And of course,
mistakenly reading my handwriting in hilarious ways. I'll
never forget such gems as: "arm-hands" and "'Jekyll tried
to and he *farted??'* 'Um, that says "failed."' 'Oh. I knew
that!'"

Contents

Chapter One - Lost in the Darkness

Sherlock Holmes,

I never expected our paths to cross again. However, at the present time I'm forced to stay in one of London's seedier regions, near a harlot house. No, you have no cause for alarm. I'm not indulging in the ladies' 'talents'; after all, who of them would have me?

I've seen something that I believe would interest you. You once commented on the singularly unique expression of determination and focus on my face when I compose music. 'Like one possessed,' I believe was your term. I have seen that same expression on a young gentleman several nights ago as he left this dreadful place. Not your normal sort to go to a house of prostitution, either. This man was too clean. Too wholesome. Of course, you can never tell what may be lurking underneath the surface. You and I both know far too well that men are masters of deceit. Indeed, especially after living in this part of the city, I have found so many more than just I have a reason to wear a mask. Though in their cases, it's not an actual covering.

To get to the main point, I believe this man is worth investigating. I do not know what his demons are, or if ones even truly exist, but his expression was too much like mine to put aside lightly. I hope we can rendezvous and investigate this together.

Erik

Erik had sufficiently raised my curiosity, so I responded immediately, requesting more information. He came to Baker Street with a plethora of it but, as with any good mystery, his responses raised more questions than answers.

"Holmes. Good to see you again," he said when I walked in to 221B the night after my reply was sent.

With a wry smile, I set down my cane, eased myself into my chair, and reached for my pipe. "Erik. Did you pick the lock on the door or the window?"

"The window. It seemed a safer way for me to gain entry. I wouldn't frighten your housekeeper half to death if she came up and saw me in the hall."

I gave a short bark of a laugh. "Mrs. Hudson? You don't expect me to believe, after just admitting to sneaking in my window, that Mrs. Hudson would see you if you didn't wish to be seen?"

Erik smiled behind his mask. "No, I suppose not. I would be safely in the shadows long before she had even an inkling I was nearby."

I struck a match and as it flared to life before my eyes, I said, "You're quite like a spider, aren't you? If for nothing more than gravity seems to have no bearing on you."

"I've compared myself to one on numerous occasions, yes."

I lit my pipe, and as tendrils of smoke began to rise, I requested, "Why not tell me of this extraordinarily focused and determined individual?"

Erik nodded and sat on the couch opposite me, stretching his long legs in front of him.

"Have you heard of a man, both a scientist and doctor, named Henry Jekyll?"

I rubbed my chin and thought through the vast library of peoples' names and professions I had in my mind. "I don't believe I'm familiar with that name, no."

Erik's eyes gave away his surprise. "I wonder if you are slipping in your knowledge of contemporary figures in science, or if he is that unknown a man."

"The latter is more likely, but I admit, either is possible. Wait a moment. Let me check my files." I caned over to my bookshelf and pulled out one of my casebooks on criminals, people of importance, and random professions that I've felt were valuable to have information on. As a matter of fact, there was a file marked "Jekyll, Henry."

"Here he is. Henry Jekyll. I don't have much. It simply says that a few years ago, he received an award in the form of a cane given to him in recognition of his achievements as a doctor and scientist. Obviously, I have failed to look over these files recently. At least, the more obscure ones."

"You have been focusing on Moriarty and those connected with him?"

"Yes. And much to my dismay, I'm not having any success."

"Have you dealt with any cases that bear his mark?"

"That's just it. There have been several, but none give me the chance to catch the one pulling the strings. I've become increasingly frustrated with the police because of this. All they care about is that the ruffians outwardly responsible are off the streets, never realizing there are scores of others just waiting to step into the fray." I sighed, then turned my attention back to the matter at hand. "Please, continue."

"Well, I initially saw this man on the thirteenth. For the next two days, I observed him and that night, wrote to you. All he seems to do is work in a laboratory he has in the basement of his residence. He's been conducting some kind of experiment and the only time I saw him leave was when he frantically raced to the pharmacist, the only man able to give him a new supply of the rare chemicals he needs."

"'Frantically raced?' That's a fascinating description."

"One deliberately chosen. He ran like a man possessed. It was almost . . ." Erik trailed off, and I could see he wanted to choose his words carefully. "It was almost as if he was running towards something, but at the same time, away from something. I had to be incredibly stealthy that night. Most people, when they have a destination in mind, don't bother to look behind them. Jekyll, on the other hand, continually glanced over his shoulder, as if expecting someone-- or something --to follow him.

"I've also seen three men and one woman continuously come and go, usually talking in the sitting room of the house, discussing their worries for Jekyll. I've been able to surmise that one man is Jekyll's butler, another a lawyer and old family friend, and the last is the father of the woman, who is Jekyll's fiancée."

"And what of this experiment? What does it pertain to? Could you discern anything concerning it?"

"Only that it has something to do with human nature. From the way two of the men were speaking, Jekyll has gone before a Board of Directors at a hospital, begging them to allow him to use a mental patient as a human subject. They've continuously refused him. From what I overheard, he's recently found a subject not sanctioned by the Board, and the butler has heard screams and the sound of someone crying in the basement late at night. Sometimes they both seem to be Jekyll's voice, but he can't be sure. It sounds too distorted. I've never heard Jekyll's voice, but I've heard the screams and cries."

"Intriguing . . ." I murmured. "Is there anything else you know?"

"Unfortunately, no. Those are the facts as I've learned them. My speculation, however, is that whatever this experiment is, it's torturing someone. You know I'm familiar with torture methods. I've no qualms about inflicting them on deserving souls, but . . . Holmes, shudders ran down *my* spine when I heard those screams. Whoever Jekyll found does *not* deserve this treatment."

I steepled my fingers in front of me, my pipe dangling from my lips. The bare particulars of this case thus far fascinated me. Erik was right to bring it to my attention. I took the pipe from my lips, doused it, and set it aside. "I must meet this man."

"I was hoping that would be your response. After all, of the two of us, you're the only one who could gain legal entry to the house."

"With my assistance, you shall, too, Erik."

He gave a sarcastic laugh. "Oh, indeed, because people are so quick to trust a man in a mask."

"They will when that man is with Sherlock Holmes," I said.

"Your arrogance shows again."

"Again? I seem to recall the first time you accused me of arrogance, you admitted your error. Besides, I prefer to think of it as confidence. Regardless, I am right. They won't say or do anything against you while you are with me. I'm sure three men and one woman will not prove too much for you. I shall introduce us and prime them for your visage. But I do ask that you be prepared, should they request it, to reveal your face."

"You would have me show them *this?"* Erik demanded, anger flashing in his eyes and he stood and threw off the mask, exposing his horribly deformed, skull-like appearance.

I barely blinked. "Erik, please. You are no longer at the opera house, no longer called a Phantom, and your face has long since lost the power to either shock or disgust me."

He sighed and took his seat. "You're right. I apologize. I still have something of a volatile temper."

"So I see. Forgiven, in any case." I picked up his facial covering. "Here is your mask. Is it made of something new?"

"Yes. A more rubbery material to better form to my features. It makes speaking, and more importantly, singing, easier."

"Indeed." I recalled Erik's beautiful singing voice. Before I let myself fall too far back in memories, however, I said, "To get back to the main point, I'd like to leave for Jekyll's immediately, but I'd prefer if Watson were with us. He may have insights you and I will miss simply because of his and Jekyll's shared profession."

"Sherlock Holmes, admitting he could miss a piece of information?" Erik asked, mockingly sarcastic.

I smiled caustically. "Whatever else I may be, I do know I'm not infallible, my dear Phantom."

"Ah, but you said moments ago I was no longer referred to as 'Phantom.' Fallible, indeed."

"Touché," I conceded.

Our playful verbal spar over, Erik said, "I have no objection to waiting. When do you expect him?"

"He is on holiday with his wife. I believe they'll return tomorrow, the eighteenth."

Erik nodded. "As I said, I have no objection. May I impose on your hospitality and stay here?"

"Of course, Erik. You needn't even ask. I'm afraid at this time I have no second bed, but I have some experiments of my own I've been tinkering with, so you can easily use mine."

"Holmes, you know me well enough by now to realize I spend most of my nights awake, composing. Besides, I should be most interested in what you're tinkering with."

I smiled. "As long as it won't bore you, I'd be glad for your input."

"I'm never bored by experiments." It was only then that he refit the mask on his face. "Do you have your violin available?"

"Always." I gestured to the violin case underneath my chemistry table. "If you would be so kind . . ."

"Of course," Erik said. He stood and retrieved the bow, rosin, and violin. As he removed the instrument from its case and began tuning it, he said to me, "Of all the subjects we've discussed, you've never explained exactly what it was that maimed your leg."

"No, I haven't," I stalled. Erik did deserve an explanation, I knew, but it was still a subject I found painful to discuss.

"Come, Detective," he said. I watched a distinct sadness melt into his eyes. "You watched as I bared my soul down in my lair. It seems only right I be privy to a piece of yours in return."

He was correct. I did owe him that much. I paused for several seconds longer, then said, "It was several months before I received the letter asking me to come to the Opera Populaire. I've been aware of Moriarty for some time now. He has a remarkable control over the lesser criminals of this city. I had tracked him to a dock on the Thames, near midnight at the start of November, where I believed I could apprehend him and bring him to justice. Instead, as Watson and I gave chase, I failed to calculate the notion that Moriarty had an accomplice in hiding. The man had a gun and shot, hoping to wound or kill either Watson or myself. Instead, the aim on his gun was off, and his bullet caught me in the right leg, shattering my femur."

Erik hissed in a breath. "I can only imagine the kind of pain that must have inflicted."

I smiled ruefully. "Is still inflicting," I corrected. "Moriarty escaped, naturally, and as I mentioned, my attempts to pick up his trail have been for naught. It's as if he simply vanished behind the criminals he controls. The gunman, I was told later, was at Watson's mercy until Watson heard me moan."

"Watson's mercy?"

"Watson knocked him into unconsciousness. I'm told the man's nose still isn't straight. Watson examined my leg and told me, to the best of his medical knowledge, that my choices were for him to operate right then to remove the bullet and bone fragments, or risk losing the entire limb."

"He operated on you on a dock on the Thames,"

Erik concluded. "Thus saving the limb, but damning you to forever having a limp, using a cane, and undoubtedly living with chronic pain."

I sighed. "Precisely."

"I'm sorry, Holmes."

"You shouldn't be."

"Why is that?"

"During as much of the recuperative process as could be achieved, I called Watson into my room and announced that because I'd taken that infernal bullet, my days as a detective were over. I could hardly climb walls or any of my usual feats when investigating a case if I couldn't even walk competently across a room unassisted. I'd decided to retire. I'd solved several smaller mysteries and I fooled myself into thinking that perhaps I could make my way in life by becoming a chemist. Or one of the run-of-the-mill scientists. I think, though I could be wrong, that it was approximately two weeks later that the managers' letter arrived, begging me to solve the mystery of their 'opera ghost.'"

"You found the story too intriguing to resist," Erik said.

"I found the *person* too intriguing to resist. I knew there was nothing supernatural happening. Everything that I hypothesized, then confirmed, about you told me that you were a human. A human whose very existence hinged upon people believing otherwise, but a human nonetheless. I knew from the start you were an extraordinary individual, and I had to meet you. That, my good fellow, was what spurred me to take the case."

Erik nodded, a slight smile showing through his naturally suspicious eyes. He'd long since finished tuning my violin and finally positioned it under his chin to begin playing a hauntingly beautiful melody. I closed my eyes and relaxed against the back of my chair, sinking into the flawless notes I could only dream of calling forth.

When he was through and I opened my eyes, he lovingly replaced the violin in its case and stared at me curiously.

"Yes?"

"I'm always fascinated by your reaction when an instrument is in my hands."

"You have such a complete mastery of them. I believe I've said something similar before, but by comparison, I feel I could produce nothing but noise. I cannot hope to produce the sounds that issue forth when you pull a bow across the strings, or place your fingers on an organ's keys."

"Perhaps you simply lack musical confidence."

"No, I just lack your ability to completely and utterly submit myself to my emotions. Yes, perhaps it could be argued that my playing is technically perfect, but that is merely the mechanics. You have perfection of mechanics and emotions."

Erik gave a self-mocking laugh. "Perfection of emotion."

"Where music is concerned."

He met my eyes and slowly nodded, knowing we both realized the immense difference. "Perhaps," was all he said.

Sherlock Holmes

In my last attempt at writing, which did turn out much better than I expected, I commented on the continuity issues I have. As I've done before, I must apologize for it. In looking back over Watson's tales, I am once again struck by how well he follows a singular line through the story, letting everything fall into it's proper place, whereas I am prone to skipping around, leaving segments incomplete, or giving entirely too much detail on things of no interest to others.

I suppose I owe it to my more patient readers, or the ones who would like more clarification of the conversation with Erik I just spoke of, to tell more of who he is and how I encountered him. About two and a half years before Erik brought Henry Jekyll to my attention, the managers of the finest opera house in Paris contacted me. They implored me to rid the opera house of a 'Phantom' who'd haunted it for months and even caused the gigantic chandelier to crash to the stage, forcing the theater to close for half a year.

As I mentioned before, I knew the culprit had to be human. What I didn't anticipate was that he was also a master musician, ventriloquist, magician, and illusionist. I had already suffered my injury and declared retirement, but the more I learned of the Opera Populaire and its history, the more I found myself unable to turn away. Once Erik and I met, we formed an, at first, uneasy alliance. After a final confrontation in Erik's lair among Erik, a soprano named Christine, and her childhood sweetheart named Raoul, Erik's and my friendship was solidified. He escaped the opera house and even stayed with me for a short period. But as was his habit, he'd disappeared into the London underground shortly after, and I hadn't heard a word from him until he sent the letter regarding Henry Jekyll.

I admit, a good deal of the reason the case caught my interest was the idea of working with Erik. I had asked him to join me as a partner after leaving the Populaire, because aside from his lack of mobility issues, he and I possess similar brilliance and deductive reasoning. But I believe now that he is a man far too accustomed to the solitary life and was far too heartbroken over the loss of Christine to even contemplate putting the barest strains of trust in anyone else. It was probable that nothing had changed by the time Jekyll came around, but I had hoped probability was wrong.

I have actually endeavored to name these chapters in this writing. One chapter may, therefore, hold several segments, because I have my own notes as well as ones from Watson, Erik, and Jekyll. Many of Jekyll's writings and such were given to me after this situation . . . ended.

So as to not give anything away before which time it should properly be revealed, I'll end off here.

In the coming pages, I give you the strange case of Dr. Jekyll . . . and Mr. Hyde.

Chapter Two - Facade

"Who, may I ask, are you?" Jekyll's butler asked when he answered the door.

"My name is Sherlock Holmes," I answered. "I am a consulting detective and these are my colleagues, Dr. John Watson, and Monsieur Erik."

"And what business do you have at this residence?" The man refused to move from the doorway, blocking us from entering. Despite being a rather small man, he had a presence about him that made him seem larger than his five-foot-five frame. Also, his elderly appearance had taken none of the sharp awareness from his pale green eyes. He regarded us, especially Erik, suspiciously.

"I assure you, we are of no threat, sir," I said. "I've spoken with John Utterson who told us we would possibly be allowed an audience with Henry Jekyll." I had contacted Utterson and he'd come to Baker Street two days before. The story he had told was extremely sad and explained much of Henry Jekyll's background. His experiment, however, remained elusive to me. I needed an audience with the one person who could explain what I needed to know. While I understood a butler's natural protectiveness for the family he serves, I found my patience for hindrances in cases had grown thin.

"They speak the truth, Poole," a voice behind us said. Erik, Watson, and I turned to see Utterson walking up. "Let us all come in out of this weather."

Still eyeing Erik, Poole did back away to let us come in out of the particularly foggy and chilly air. When we were seated in the parlor, near an exquisite fireplace with a life-size painting of an older man above the mantel, Poole brought us drinks and commented, "I don't see how bringing in outsiders will help Henry."

"You have never read the stories Dr. Watson has published in the *Strand*, I assume?" Utterson said. "Sherlock Holmes is a genius who can piece together the most minute tapestry of clues. If anyone can discern why Henry is behaving as he is, it is this man."

Watson seemed immensely impressed that Utterson should think so highly of me based on his own writings. I, however, viewed things differently.

"Mr. Utterson, I thank you for your over-inflated sense of confidence in me. However, I assure you, it *is* over-inflated. While I can, and have, pieced together intricate tapestries of clues, they are not, as Watson's writings suggest, done in a matter of hours or days." I glanced at Erik. "In fact, I met Erik on one such case. It took a month or more before a conclusion could be reached."

The two men looked shocked, so I felt I had to continue. "I will do my absolute best to quickly delve into whatever Henry Jekyll is doing. But if you wish to place time constraints on me, I'm afraid you need to find a new man."

"The only issue of time is that in approximately six weeks, Henry is to marry to Miss Emma Carew," Poole said. "She may, understandably, wish you to solve this before their wedding."

"Ah, yes. That would most definitely be a concern." I leaned forward and said to Utterson, "Well, that is an understandable time constraint and I promise you, I will do my best. Please, start at the beginning. Tell me anything you can about Henry Jekyll and why his recent behavior disturbs you."

"But you sought me out for these details two days ago," he said.

"Yes, but my companions were not with me. Please, reiterate for their benefit."

"Very well. I have been friends with the Jekyll family for some thirty years, back when I first began to practice law. Henry's father was my intial client, and thus began a lifelong friendship.

"When Henry was first born, I was as proud as if he was my own son. I watched him grow into a fine young man, but as he grew . . . his father seemed to deteriorate. The man would stare off into space for hours at a time. At first, it seemed he was just daydreaming, and anyone calling his name could pull him back to us. But as the months, then years passed, he stopped responding to all but Henry. Finally, about seven years ago, he stopped reacting even to his son. He gave no verbal replies to anything, nor any physical sign of acknowledgement, and eventually gave no notice of hearing anything said to him. It was as if he was trapped in his own world, or so Henry believed. Henry was unable to care for him day and night, though for a short period he did try. His attempt failed and his father was placed in a mental institution. But Henry still visited him faithfully. He became obsessed with the idea that his father's mind was still whole, but that something was blocking his ability to express himself."

"Almost a concept of 'mind over brain,'" I murmured. "I apologize. Do go on."

"Henry, when his father began rapidly declining, began working with different chemicals in an effort to find some way to save the man. Make his mind whole, I believe. For the past seven years, Henry has been trying to convince the St. Jude Board of Governors to allow him a subject upon which to test his theories. Despite Henry's stories of success with rodents, the Board has continually denied him, calling his experiments unethical, dangerous, and presumptuous. They've accused him of riding roughshod over lines a scientist and doctor should not cross, and the more insistently they refused, the more it infuriated Henry. He is determined to save his father and can't understand how they would deny him when he is so sure his experiments will save many lives."

"And what has he said of this experiment of his? Has he ever described to you what it entails?"

Utterson and Poole looked at one another and Utterson said, "I've heard precious little. It has something to do with human nature and the duality of man. Sir Danvers Carew would be the better man to inquire about such things. He is part of the Board and the only man who did not reject Henry."

"What was his vote?" Watson asked.

"He abstained," Utterson answered.

"I've something to add, sirs," Poole interjected.

"Yes?" I said, turning my attention to the butler.

"Master Jekyll had come home late one night, a bit over a week ago. He briefly asked me what his father's personality was like years ago, before this affliction. And he asked if his father's will was strong."

"What did you reply?"

"The truth, sir. The man possessed an incredibly

strong will and a personality like none other. He was the finest man I've ever known."

"Once again, I'm fascinated by this," I said. "Now that all three of us have something of an understanding of Henry Jekyll's life, may we speak with him directly?"

"I'm unsure, sir." Poole said. "He instructed me this morning that he would be in his laboratory all day and that no one was to disturb him." At a look from Utterson, he sighed heavily, turned, and as he walked away, we heard him muttering, "I suppose I'll find out if that's still the case."

Once he was gone, Utterson cleared his throat. "I apologize in advance if this is a sensitive issue, Monsieur Erik, but why are you masked? You are not a wanted man, are you?"

I let out a short bark of laughter at the irony in his question. Though Utterson gave me a sidelong glance, he kept his attention on Erik.

Erik avoided his second question by responding, "I merely have a severe facial deformity that most find unbearable to gaze upon."

"Ah. I'm sorry for my intrusion into your privacy, then."

Behind the mask, Erik's eyes showed intense surprise and gratitude. *"Merci, monsieur,"* was his quiet reply.

I saw Watson put a reassuring hand on Erik's shoulder just as Poole reappeared. "I'm sorry, sirs, but Master Jekyll insists he cannot be disturbed by anyone today."

"Very well," I said, standing with the assistance of my cane. Watson and Erik rose as well. "Is there a more convenient time I can come back to speak with him?"

"I'm unsure, Mr. Holmes."

"I'll simply come back in a day or two. If I am fortunate, he will see me."

"Yes, sir."

As we were shown out the door, Erik and I exchanged a smile.

From the Journal of John H. Watson, M.D.

As we left the Jekyll household, I witnessed Holmes and Erik exchange a peculiar smile. I'd seen the same expression on Holmes's face numerous times before, and knew they'd both observed something to which I was completely oblivious.

"What do you make of it, Watson? Erik?" Holmes asked as we hailed a hansom and got out of the ever-foggy air to return to Baker Street.

"Poole may know more than he's willing to reveal in front of a masked man," Erik volunteered immediately. "Or, as a butler, he has that immense of a sense of loyalty to Jekyll and his behavior and secrets."

"Yes, I received that impression as well," Holmes agreed.

"If Jekyll's father is truly his motivation, however, that seems a logical place to begin our investigation," Erik added.

"Holmes, that's right," I said. In regard to the senior Jekyll, whatever did you mean when you said 'mind over brain?'"

"Simple, my good man. Jekyll Senior's thoughts and emotions wish for some kind of release, or ability to be released, which his brain, the mechanics of it, is unable to provide."

"Holmes," Erik said, "you and I seem to have arrived at the same conclusion. You don't suppose . . . ?"

"I'm afraid I do."

Though I gave them extremely confused glances, both men fell into contemplative silence, and neither spoke until we were back in 221B.

Erik went straight to what seemed to be his favoured spot by the window behind Holmes's desk. I perched on the couch, waiting for one or the other to explain their shared conclusion, but Erik only stared, and Holmes caned over to sit in his favourite armchair and light his pipe. The ticking clock began to grind on my nerves and finally, I could stand the silence no longer.

"Explain yourselves!" I exclaimed. "I admit to not having the mental fortitude of the likes of you, but please explain your conclusion so I'm not completely lost and may offer my opinion!"

Both men turned surprised eyes on me.

"I do apologize, Watson," Holmes said. "I truly thought this was a clear enough process of logic."

"Not in my case," I muttered.

"Allow me," Erik interjected. "We learned of Jekyll's father. A man in a mental institution. Utterly forgotten by society and unable even to communicate anymore. Jekyll's need for a subject, finding one not sanctioned by the Board . . ."

"Dear God . . . You believe he kidnapped his own father in order to experiment on him?"

"Men have done far stranger and more desperate things," Erik said, adding darkly, "I should know."

"However, we must not accept this as absolute fact," Holmes said. "True, this theory appears to fit the data, but our minds must remain open."

"Open? But how, Holmes?" I asked, still stricken.

"By gaining more data before we theorize." But something in my expression must have stopped him, for he continued, "All right. I suppose it would behoove us to

26

see where this theory may take us."

"It--it's despicable!" I sputtered. "Using his father for an experiment when the man is unable to consent? It goes against everything a doctor stands for! This man must be nothing but a lunatic!"

"Lunatic? That's quite a rash conclusion to come to, Watson. Sanity is actually quite subjective."

"How is that?" I demanded, indignant that my horror was being under-rated.

"You meet someone. Someone obsessive about his hobbies. Someone who likes finding the unorthodox methods and solutions. A person who spends his time with dangerous chemicals, and is prone to clouds of melancholia consuming him. Occasionally during these periods, he takes cocaine solutions. He's also a free shot with a rifle, indoors. Would you want to associate with this man?"

Not realizing the trap I was falling into, I said, "I would have to consider for quite some time before making that decision."

Giving me a grin, he said, "You didn't have to think about it very long before deciding to share Baker Street with that man."

I sputtered for several minutes, not knowing what to say.

Holmes gave me an amused glance. "As I said, sanity is subjective." Steepling his fingers in front of his chest, he asked, "And what do you think, Erik?"

"It is a reasonable assumption. Poole mentioned the screams that sounded like Jekyll, yet distorted."

"Indeed," Holmes agreed. "However, he could not have taken his father alone. Watson's opinion would not be original, so I can't imagine the one Jekyll would have found as an accomplice."

Erik made a strange murmuring sound in the back of his throat. "I can."

"Erik?"

"I apologize, Holmes, but there is a detail I've forgotten until now."

"What is that?" Holmes asked. I had to wonder if Erik picked up on the trace amount of annoyance in Holmes's tone. I knew it irked him immensely if even the smallest details were excluded in a case's summarization.

"Just after Jekyll exited the premises, a young unfortunate caught up with him. I didn't hear their conversation, but I watched him pass her what I can only assume was his business card."

"An unfortunate used to retrieve someone whom society has deemed a madman."

"It fits the timeframe. That hard, determined expression came over his face after they separated. Before she caught up to him, he merely looked thoughtful," Erik clarified.

"Hmm. It also fits what Poole said about Jekyll coming home late and asking about the strength of his father's will. He must have run into that woman the same night, made his decision, and asked Poole about his father."

"So, he has his victim, he has an accomplice, and he's given her a way to contact him," I said. "And of course, if she tried to turn on him, who would believe her story? Even if someone bothered to listen, she would be immediately discredited because of who she is and because he's a distinguished member of society. But why ask about his father unless that's who his intended victim was?"

"Simple," Holmes said. "There are two possibilities concerning that. One is that yes, Jekyll Senior was the victim. The other is that Jekyll wanted to know if some of his father's strength also runs through his own veins. If he would have the mental fortitude to remain on the course he's chosen."

Erik nodded in agreement and Holmes said, "All right. I believe we've successfully theorized on this possibility long enough. We need more information on Jekyll Senior."

"Allow me to be of assistance in this matter," I said. "I shall visit the mental institution and discover all I can about Jekyll's father."

Holmes and Erik exchanged an amused glance and I sighed in exasperation, knowing once again that there was something vital I was missing. "What is it now?"

"Which institution is he in?" Holmes asked.

My mind drew a blank. It had never been said.

"Damnation," I muttered. "Can I be of no assistance to you?"

Holmes chuckled and even Erik smiled. "Of course you can, Watson. If nothing else, by the humour you unwittingly provide. Check into St. Jude," Holmes suggested. "If his father had to be put away, I can think of no better board to appeal to than the one that governs the hospital where one's father is placed."

I nodded, hopelessly trying to maintain the façade that I would have arrived at that conclusion sooner or later.

"Besides Jekyll's father as the victim, what other

hypotheses can we draw from the information at hand?" Holmes posed the question as he refilled his pipe.

I could come up with nothing. I found myself paralyzed by the horror of our first hypothesis. Well, I should say 'theirs.' It struck me once again that this was Holmes's, and subsequently Erik's, main advantage over the rest of society. Both were so easily able to put aside human emotion and focus purely on the puzzle at hand.

"Even if there are no others at this point, we should gather further information," Erik said.

Holmes nodded. "That goes without saying. We shall each have specific jobs in what may turn out to be the coming days. Watson, you find any information available on the father. Start with St. Jude. Erik, you take me to where you saw that woman catch up with Jekyll. Then, go back to his residence and see if you can find an alternate way into the basement."

"An alternate way? Holmes, do you wish to bypass Poole so much that you will break into a house?"

"No, of course not. It's just unlikely that anyone Jekyll would experiment on would be brought through the front door."

"Of course," I muttered, once again feeling foolish.

"I wonder if it is something else, or if he does have that much obsessive devotion toward his father."

"It is too fine a line to walk for long, Holmes."

"Why do you say that, Erik?" I asked.

"One day, you are obsessively devoted, the next. ."

"You are kidnapping a chorus girl and bringing her to your lair," Holmes finished slowly. "Yes, your point is well made."

I nodded in agreement, though I'm sure the

magnitude of what Erik got across to Holmes was partially lost on me. However, we all agreed to follow Holmes's suggestion and go on our assignments the next day.

Erik rang for Mrs. Hudson to bring us some much needed tea.

Chapter Three - Pursue the Truth

I must admit, I have a large amount of respect for Holmes's methods. Then there's the additional benefit that even in a mask, others will, however grudgingly, accept me when I walk beside Sherlock Holmes.

The following morning, as Watson prepared for his trip to St. Jude, Holmes readied himself by dirtying his face, and smudging grime down his cheekbones and under his eyes, as well as underneath his fingernails and on his knuckles. Dressed in filthy, torn clothing appropriate for the East End's seediest region, he was even able to give his cane a shabby, worn appearance. It never ceased to amaze me how he could transform himself into nearly any part his detective's skills called for. I was especially glad to see him in a disguise like this. It signified a boost in Holmes's confidence, because when I initially came to Baker Street, Watson once confided in me that when Holmes was at the opera house, he hadn't felt he could competently disguise himself because his cane gave away too much.

We took a hansom cab to within four blocks of the establishment. Holmes insisted on walking the remaining distance, so I led him to the ramshackle building I'd resided in for longer than I cared to remember, and pointed out the whore house next to it.

"The Red Rat," he murmured. "And Jekyll was in there?"

"For no more than an hour, I'm assuming. As I mentioned, he doesn't seem the type. See the lamppost by the corner, there? That's where the girl caught up to him."

"And where were you?"

"In the alley nearby, waiting for the rare moment when no one is outside so I could get back to my room."

"All right. Shall we reconvene in three hours, then?"

"I don't imagine it will take me that long."

"But it may take me that long. Remember, I'll be trying to get this woman to confide in me. I can't see an unfortunate being overly trusting. Especially not when I look like this," Holmes gestured down at himself, then continued. "Also, Jekyll could be craftier than we're expecting. Never underestimate an opponent. That's what made the managers at the opera house such fools. They continually thought they could outwit you because they did not understand the opponent they faced."

"Indeed. Point well taken." I held out my hand. "Baker Street in three hours, then?"

He shook mine in agreement and then I watched him cross the road and enter the Red Rat.

I didn't bother hailing a hansom cab; instead, I took to the alleyways and other back roads until I found myself at Jekyll's. As with the previous times I'd been there, I was struck by the distinct difference between the front and side of the house. The front area was immaculate; the lawn flawlessly trimmed, a new coat of paint recently applied, and no shutters were even loose, let alone broken or creaking on rusted hinges.

But by comparison, the further one went toward the back of the house, the more it looked like a dilapidated ruin. The paint peeled, shutters were missing, and down almost at ground level was a boarded-up window below some freshly trimmed bushes. It seemed only the area facing the street, (and therefore society,) was up kept immaculately clean and in good repair. It was assuredly something to mention to Holmes. I couldn't help wondering, however, if Jekyll was truly that obsessed with keeping up appearances?

Wait a moment . . . a ground level window? I had a feeling I'd found exactly what I came to search for. Stealthily approaching it, I moved branches of the bush out of the way and quickly determined the wood was almost rotted through. It would take little time and almost no noise to remove it. However, because of its fragility, I doubted my ability to move it in one piece.

Getting to my hands and knees, I knelt down and put my ear inches away from the wood. At first, I could hear nothing. But then there was a crash and a strangled scream. My eyebrows furrowed together as I tried to discern if this could be the scream of an older mental patient. But then, a voice spoke, chilling even me with its tone of pure, animalistic hatred. Just three words, but they were enough to render me motionless.

"Jekyll, you fool!"

I heard the unmistakable sounds of chains rattling and that spurred my bones to function again. I'd found a potential way in to Jekyll's laboratory and I'd heard the voice of his victim. Backing away from the window, I glanced at my pocket watch and saw only three quarters of an hour had passed since Holmes and I separated. But I needed to think and since Baker Street had become something of a sanctuary for me lately, I fled there to gather my thoughts.

*****

Watson arrived last at Baker Street. When Holmes came in, he noted my expression but said nothing, for which I was grateful. Fixing his pipe with fresh tobacco, he joined me in silence for the next hour. When the three of us sat down and began talking, we found there was an interesting plethora of information to sort through. I was just as glad that Watson volunteered his findings first. That scream and those three words still haunted my mind. Despite my best efforts, I found it increasingly difficult to focus on his words. By the time I was fully able to, his tale was almost finished and I was left to play catch-up.

"Gone? What do you mean, gone?" I heard Holmes ask.

"Vanished. Disappeared. No longer present," Watson clarified needlessly. "Jekyll's father had indeed been institutionalized at St. Jude, but he's not there anymore, and any papers about his stay, his condition, they're gone."

"Impossible, then, that if the senior Jekyll is the subject of the experiment, that this was decided on a whim," Holmes said. "Lucy can't have been an accomplice."

"Lucy?" I asked.

"The unfortunate to whom you saw Jekyll give his card."

"You found her."

"Yes."

"Holmes," Watson interjected. "We may have another suspect for Jekyll's experiment."

"Oh? And who is that?"

"Erik, you mentioned that one of the people

worried about Jekyll's well-being was his fiancée's father. His name is Sir Danvers Carew. I met him at St. Jude."

"Yes, Utterson mentioned him and said he was the better person to ask what Jekyll's experiment consisted of. What information did he give you? Because I highly doubt you are suggesting he is the victim."

"Heavens, no. He gave me precious little until I introduced myself and said I was helping your investigation into Jekyll's strange behavior. After that, he warmed up to me and told me a bit about his daughter's relationship to Jekyll. He also mentioned a man named Simon Stride."

"Who is he?"

"Apparently, he was a suitor of Emma's just before she met Jekyll. And Sir Danvers explained to me how very bitter Stride is over Emma's rejection. Stride even allegedly threatened Jekyll, saying that because Jekyll stole the girl who should rightfully be his, Jekyll would pay with his life."

"Allegedly? Sir Danvers did not hear it directly, I take it," Holmes said.

"Precisely. Either Emma or Jekyll told him shortly after the event."

"But if the threat is true, or Stride was a serious contender to the stability of Jekyll's relationship with Emma, he may have wished to rid himself of the competition," I said. "Which would mean Stride is the one suffering."

"And it lends credence to the notion that Jekyll has crossed over into insanity," Holmes added. "Obsessed devotion is one thing; vengeful jealousy is quite another."

"Yes, it is. And I'm afraid I only have grim news

to report, as well."

"Oh, Erik? And what is that?"

I explained briefly about the dual appearance of Jekyll's house and about the boarded-up window under the bushes. "The worst part was when I knelt to see if I could hear anything from his laboratory."

"You heard his victim," Holmes concluded.

I nodded. "An anguished scream and then the single coldest, fiercest-sounding voice saying *'Jekyll, you fool!'* And I can't be sure that this was the situation, but it sounded like the man was chained to a wall."

"To prevent escape?" Watson asked.

"Possible." Holmes lit his pipe and I watched the glow from the match reflect in his eyes, which were narrowed in a singularly dangerous expression. "We must meet with Jekyll. Tomorrow. Poole will not stand in our way."

From the Journal of John H. Watson, M.D.

We set out for Jekyll's home around noontime. Holmes explained that if Jekyll was truly anything like a normal English gentleman, he would break in his experiment for lunch. Arriving at the house at approximately half-past, it was Utterson who answered the door.

"Holmes, Dr. Watson, Erik, I'm glad to see you," he murmured quietly, ushering us into the parlor.

"Something has happened. What is it, Utterson?" Holmes asked.

Utterson's legs seemed to lose all their strength and he collapsed and very nearly fell off of an armchair Adjusting his position, he said, "Henry requested I get these drugs and chemicals for him from the pharmacist. He said he dared not leave here. When I delivered them shortly before you arrived, he seized them from me and escaped back down to his laboratory." He held out a list of what I assumed were the requested chemicals to Holmes. Holmes took it, muttering to himself as he perused it.

"Hmm. Utterson, why did this reaction distress you so greatly?"

"I'm . . . unsure, to be honest. All I know is that I've never seen Henry appear so out of control. He is normally such an independent, motivated, calm man. To have him say he dared not leave, it struck a chord of great discomfort in me."

Holmes nodded. "Another question. Escaped, you said. Why use that word?"

"Because that's what he did, Mr. Holmes. I admit, I'm not fond of going down to Henry's laboratory; I told him I would get his supplies only if he would greet me here. He obliged, but as soon as the containers were in his hands, he fled, as if he couldn't get away from me fast enough."

"And this isn't normal behavior for him," Holmes speculated.

"Indeed not, sir," Utterson confirmed. "Henry would normally converse with me for some time. Yet since coming to whatever decision he has about these experiments, he has become secretive, solitary. He's forgetting about all other aspects of his life. He is becoming his work and nothing more."

"Utterson, we must come face-to-face with Henry Jekyll," Holmes said.

"I will oblige you as best I can, but if he refuses, what more can we do?"

"I'm unsure, but I can usually be counted on to think up contingency plans." He gave the list one last glance and asked, "Might I keep this? I'm something of a chemist and given enough time to examine the components involved, I may be able to gain some insight into what exactly his experiment is."

"Do not keep the original list. I have no doubt Henry will ask for that back, once he remembers that I have it. But you are free to copy it. Allow me to find pen and paper."

Utterson went to look for those as Holmes resumed studying the list. When Utterson returned, Holmes carefully copied whatever it said to a new sheet and gave the first back to Utterson. "Now, may we see about

Jekyll?"

Utterson, suppressing a shudder, left the room. Holmes caned his way over to the fireplace and stared up at the immense painting. "I wonder . . ." he murmured.

"Holmes?" I said questioningly.

"I believe Jekyll had this painting commissioned to remind himself of what his father used to be. Normally the subject of the piece has it done, but not in this case."

"Why are you so sure?" I asked, even though I saw Erik give a small smile, having no doubt already discerned Holmes's method.

Holmes looked at me and then pointed to the lower right hand corner of the painting. "The artist signed and dated it. It was begun and completed only five years ago."

Erik nodded and I was once again left feeling that my observational skills were extremely inadequate. Before I could voice any such insecurity, though, Utterson returned. The three of us faced him and his expression became distinctly uncomfortable.

"Erik, I apologize, but Henry's condition for meeting with Mr. Holmes was that just he and Dr. Watson be present."

Erik's disappointment and sudden rage were almost palpable. Because of Holmes's descriptions and my own experience of how isolated Erik has been throughout his years, I knew I couldn't truly understand his feelings. But I still put my hand on his shoulder in a physical show of support. Unfortunately, I knew there was nothing I could say. There were no words that would truly reassure him.

Utterson must have noticed as well, because he said, "Monsieur Erik, please do not misunderstand. It is nothing against you. Henry simply doesn't know you. Mr. Holmes and Dr. Watson, he has at least heard of, thanks to Dr. Watson's publications."

If Erik believed him, I couldn't tell. Giving Erik's shoulder a final squeeze, I followed Utterson quietly down the hallway. I heard Holmes behind me say, "I will recall every detail for you," and then follow himself. We went down a flight of tight, circular stairs and at their end was a large wooden door.

"Henry?" Utterson called, going up to the door. "I did as you asked. It is only Dr. Watson and Mr. Holmes with me."

"Leave us, Utterson. I'll speak with them alone," was the muffled reply.

Utterson nodded to us and ascended the spiral staircase.

"Jekyll?" Holmes called.

The door opened a crack. All I could see within was inky blackness.

"Jekyll?" Holmes repeated. The door didn't move, though I observed Holmes placing his cane in that inch of space so the door could not be suddenly closed on us. In a friendlier tone, he said, "Henry? Please. We only wish to help you. Let us in."

The door yawned open before us a minute later, but only after we'd stepped in and the door was shut did Henry Jekyll show himself.

Recently, a woman named Mary Shelley wrote a novel entitled *Frankenstein.* I've yet to read it, but my understanding is that Victor Frankenstein is nothing more than a mad scientist who, through electricity, brings a man back from the dead. I had built up a mental image of

Henry Jekyll to match the one my mind created for a mad scientist, based on the idea of Victor Frankenstein. Dirty white lab coat, sagging trouser socks, trousers either thinned or ripped at the knee, a wild, untamed expression in his eyes, and salt and pepper hair that stuck out at odd angles.

The Henry Jekyll that stood before us in the dim light had none of those characteristics. His slightly longer, dark hair was pulled back in a respectably neat fashion, his shirt was clean and pressed, his trousers immaculate, he wore no lab coat, nor did I see one in the room, and his eyes, though they darted around nervously, had a kind look about them.

"Thank you, Henry. As you know, I'm Sherlock Holmes, and this is--"

"Yes, yes, I'm quite aware of who you are, Mr. Holmes. I've read several of your monographs." He turned his attention to me. "And Dr. Watson, I greatly enjoyed A Study in Scarlet. Very good read."

"Thank you."

"Which of my monographs have you read?"

"'Upon the Distinction between the Ashes of the Various Tobaccos,' two on poisons, and most recently, I read your article 'The Book of Life.'"

Inwardly, I cringed. I recalled when I first saw that article. It was during the case Jekyll complimented me on. I was waiting for Mrs. Hudson to bring up my breakfast and I picked up a magazine, where I saw a piece in which the author insisted that through careful observation of the smallest details, one could discover the innermost thoughts of another. I believed it to be rubbish and exclaimed to Holmes that it was nothing more than ineffable twaddle.

Imagine my embarrassment when he told me he was the author!

"Ah, 'The Book of Life.' Was it to your liking?"

"I'm unsure 'liking' is the proper term. I found it fascinating, however. While I'm quite certain I'm nowhere close to the caliber you are, I've begun my own practice of paying attention to the small details of others to see what I can discern."

"Indeed?" Holmes said, traces of curiosity and surprised laced within his skepticism. "Would you care to show me your skills?"

Jekyll's face turned pink. "I'm certain I will only embarrass myself, but all right. I'll give it a try."

Holmes stood, facing Jekyll, arms away from his sides, palms towards the ceiling with his cane resting gently across them, parallel to the floor. Jekyll approached and looked Holmes in the eye. Then his gaze went down Holmes's neck, down one sleeve to his right hand, across the cane to his left, and up that arm, where he stopped to lightly touch Holmes's shoulder. He looked over Holmes's torso and down both of his legs to his shoes before standing back and saying, "I have your word that you will give me the truth as well as any falsehoods in my assessment?"

"Of course. Anyone using my methods should use them properly. I have no wish to steer you wrong."

"Very good, then. In that case, you're a very secretive man. You value privacy and count on others being unobservant, yet you're not lazy with the things you wish to guard. What I mean is, you're not dependent upon others' lack of observational acuity. The cane is not ornamental. You use it for needed balance assistance because your right . . . foot? is somehow afflicted. It's an older injury, because your coat has a slight tear in the upper right forearm, probably because you stumbled. I can't be sure since I cannot see the bottoms of your shoes, but I feel your right foot was injured because you seem to walk more heavily on your left, and that would mean that shoe was worn down more than its mate."

Holmes looked at him with respect. "Very good, Henry. I must admit, for someone new to this, you are very observant. Of course, you have several things partially or outright wrong, yet they've given you support for the things that were correct.

"First, yes, I do value my privacy and your assumption about my lack of dependency on others' observational deficiencies is correct. Second, yes, this cane is a needed accessory. Third, while it is my right side, it was my thigh that took the injury. There was irrevocable muscle damage. Fourth, while it is an older injury, the slight tear on my sleeve came after I snagged it on the window inside my dwelling about eight months ago. Given its position, the tear is in no danger of growing, so I've simply neglected having it fixed. Fifth, yes, I walk with a rather pronounced limp, so I'm quite sure you're correct and my left sole is much more worn than my right."

Jekyll gave an embarrassed smile as Holmes resumed his regular standing position: cane down, his weight on it and his left leg. "Was there anything I missed?"

"Oh, many things. More proof the cane was needed would be the callous on my right hand. Then, there are the scars and pock-marks on my palms and fingers which would tell you I also dabble in chemistry. If you want something more mundane, neither Watson nor I washed our faces after breakfast this morning, so you could tell by looking at the corners of my mouth that I ate a buttered roll with breakfast, as I can tell that from Watson."

I hastily tried to discreetly wipe my mouth.

Holmes smiled. "But these are mostly trivial things. You did rather well for someone with little experience."

"Thank you," Jekyll said.

Nodding, Holmes caned his way towards an extremely large table with a chemistry set on it that dwarfed his own. Awe in his voice, he said, "You're quite the chemist, Henry. And anyone who has so much to offer about my monographs obviously does more than dabble. I've never seen so extensive a set."

"I'm humbled, Mr. Holmes. I'd invite you to have a more hands-on examination of things, but I'm afraid I must insist you only look. I'm in the middle of something that cannot be disturbed or altered in the slightest."

"Indeed," Holmes murmured again, glancing from test tube to Bunsen burner. "Utterson, your fiancée and her father, and your butler are all very worried about you."

"As they've said to me repeatedly."

"I was told you've declined their repeated attempts at visits."

"Poole has given me their messages."

"Yet you refuse to respond in kind."

"My work keeps me very busy. I must remain constantly vigilant. Outside influences cannot be allowed to distract me."

Holmes's jaw clenched. "Outside influences? You would categorize your fiancée as nothing more than that?"

Sighing, Jekyll said, "Unfortunately, right now that is the case. I must isolate myself; if I don't, something may go terribly wrong."

Holmes turned a stern eye on him. His annoyance was swift and I didn't understand the source. "Jekyll, what is the nature of this experiment that has your loved ones so worried? Who have you found that the Board refused to sanction?"

Jekyll moved towards his chemistry table and wrapped his fingers protectively around a leather-bound book. A journal of his works, I assumed. Perhaps a log of how this most recent experiment was progressing. His eyes flashed angrily. "You have overstepped your bounds, Mr. Holmes. What I do in the privacy of my own residence is none of your concern. Neither are any details of my work or my volunteer. I think you and Dr. Watson should take your leave." Clutching the journal in a guarded fashion, he reached for the door with his other hand and pointedly stared at us and then out the doorway.

To my surprise, Holmes immediately acquiesced. Back to his niceties, he said, "Jekyll, my concern is for you. Word has reached my ear of nothing short of troubling activities on your part and I only wish to help you. I pray you can understand that."

Jekyll met Holmes's eyes, but turned away a moment later. "I do understand that. But right now, no one can help me."

Nodding slowly, Holmes merely said, "Come, let us take our leave, Watson."

We ascended the stairs, hearing the laboratory door close heavily behind us. When we reached the sitting room, Poole and Utterson were huddled near the mantelpiece, their faces drawn and pale. Erik, his face turned away from them, stood on the opposite side of the room.

Holmes appeared to take no notice and announced, "Gentlemen, I'm afraid I didn't get far beyond an introduction. However, it has given me several things to consider. I shall come again for an audience with Jekyll, but it won't be for several days."

Poole and Utterson merely nodded, still looking shaken. I couldn't help but ponder what could possibly have rattled their cages so greatly.

When the three of us left the Jekyll household and we were safely in a hansom cab on the way back to Baker Street, Holmes let out a deep sigh and tapped his index finger on his cane. "Erik, why did you show them your face?"

My eyes widened. *"That* is why they looked so unnerved?"

"Indeed," Homes answered. "I said I would prepare them and that you may have to remove your mask *if necessary."*

"Poole did not believe I had a facial deformity. I chose to prove him wrong," Erik said shortly.

Shaking his head, Holmes asked, "But did you have to do it in a manner meant to terrify?"

"This is why I refused a partnership between us, Holmes. I know no other ways but torture, mayhem, and terror."

Holmes locked eyes with Erik for a long moment

and nothing could be heard save for the wheels of the cab and the steady clip-clop of the horse's hooves on the cobblestones below. Finally, Holmes looked away. I thought at first Erik had won their battle of wills. But then, and I'm sure if my inadequate sense of hearing could decipher these words, Erik had no trouble, Holmes murmured, "Yes, you do."

Chapter Four - Take Me As I Am

September 22nd, 10:00 pm

    The experiments are in their second week. To make things more complicated, somehow Sherlock Holmes, Dr. Watson, and a third man have been summoned. It was difficult enough to keep the details a secret when it was only Poole, Utterson, Emma, and Sir Danvers concerned for my well-being. Concern, I can handle, even in the state I seem to be rapidly approaching. Dogged curiosity, the likes of which Mr. Holmes possesses, I pray does not prove too much for me. I had hoped allowing them to see me would allay any questions Mr. Holmes had. Instead, he seems to have increased his interest tenfold.

    I feel now I may have been tricked by letting him into my laboratory, because I mentioned my familiarity with his 'Book of Life' monograph. He asked me to put his methods to the test to see what conclusions I could draw about him. I believe I did passably, but that pride, that need to impress the master of these methods, will it cost me? For I did not ask him to return the favor and let me be privy to what he observed.

Added to that is the fact that today, as I was coming back to my house after receiving the last of the new chemicals I desperately need, Emma was waiting at the door. I wanted to, oh, I wanted to escape inside without speaking to her, but I couldn't. She has been so good to me, supporting me even as I shun her company and yes, even her love. I know I do not deserve her, yet I am and ever shall be forever grateful she has not forsaken me. I know I do not, **can not**, show it right now, but I love her.

Dear God, I love Emma Carew.

Sherlock Holmes

"Mr. Holmes?" Mrs. Hudson said as she gently opened the door.

"Yes?"

"You have a visitor. A young lady named Emma."

"Ah, very good. Show her in, please."

Mrs. Hudson backed up several steps and a young lady with ringlets of blonde hair pinned at the nape of her neck and wearing a navy blue high-collared dress stepped inside. "Hello, Mr. Holmes."

"Hello, Miss Carew. I'm pleased to meet you, but I must admit, I wasn't expecting your company."

"I know. I apologize for coming here without an invitation, but I was told you're the man who will figure out what is plaguing Henry."

"Yes, I hope to. Please, take a seat and tell me in detail why you've come."

She perched on the edge of the couch. "I've just had a rather odd conversation with Henry. He was on his way back from getting more rare chemicals for his experiment and I was . . . fortunate . . . enough to be at his door when he returned."

"More rare chemicals? I was there earlier this afternoon and Utterson said he had just come from procuring what was on Jekyll's list."

"I know nothing about that, Mr. Holmes. I just know what I observed."

I nodded. "You hesitated when you said 'fortunate.' Why?"

Slowly, she said, "I'm not certain fortune would have placed me in so odd a talk. Mr. Holmes, I'm not even certain how to describe it."

I leaned forward, all the more curious. "Please, madam, try."

"He was . . . frenzied. Almost like he wished to speak to no one. While I suppose that is nothing new, it still . . . I'm unsure. Unsettled me, I suppose would be the best way to say it. There was an urgency about him that *is* new. Henry is -- or was -- a very calm, meticulous man who does an extensive amount of planning before deciding on a course."

"So he's not someone to make rash decisions?"

"Not at all. Though once he's found that course and examined every angle, the only way he knows is straight ahead."

"He won't be swayed to a new goal, then? Or perhaps a different path to achieve the same goal?"

"Not in the time I've known him. And in case you want to know, that's been just over three years."

"Yes, I was going to ask. Thank you. Miss Carew, there is something else I'd like your help with, that may or may not concern Henry."

"Really? What is it?"

"Tell me about Simon Stride."

She gave an involuntary gasp. "Simon?"

"Yes. Allegedly, he recently threatened Henry Jekyll."

"Henry did mention that. Simon was just making Henry feel worse, I think, after being rejected by the Board."

"Simon allegedly threatened him the same day that

his proposal was formally rejected?"

"Yes. To my understanding, Simon is nothing more than a record-keeper for the Board of Governors. It is my opinion that he was bitter over not being able to vote in saying no to Henry."

"So issuing even an empty threat may have satisfied the man?"

"Quite possibly."

"Just for my own clarification, I understand you and Mr. Stride have a history. Is it possible his threat to Henry had something to do with you?"

"Well . . ." Emma's cheeks turned pink with embarrassment. "It's . . . possible, I suppose. He . . . he was my beau. I was . . . fond of him, I must confess, and he spoke of adoring me. But as time passed, it became apparent that I was not the kind of woman he would be satisfied with."

"Why is that?"

"Most young women today are weak and demure things, dictated to by a man as to how to behave. Simon wants a woman on his arm he can parade around. Someone incomplete whom he can make feel whole. Someone sweet, young, and nothing if not obedient to him. As I told him recently when he was trying to talk me out of my engagement to Henry, I am not that woman."

"A rare mindset for a woman of today," I commented.

"Yes. My father, however, has always encouraged a strong sense of independence in me. He made sure I learned that if I was not happy with something, that I speak up, or walk away. I have to be careful how often I exert this sense of self, because to most, it is a very unorthodox and subsequently, quite disturbing thing."

"Not so much to me. I've come across other women of stature who have their own minds and hearts and have no such trouble expressing their dislike of a situation. I believe it is a very forward-thinking notion, rather than to assume that women are the 'weaker sex' and therefore unable to handle the same mental strains as a man."

She smiled at me. "That's exactly what my father said once. Forward-thinking. He wanted me to be ready, because it seemed to him that things in the world were going to change. Unfortunately, Simon is not one for changes such as those. As I said, I told Simon recently I was not his perfectly submissive woman he could claim for a wife. But when I reiterated it . . ."

"Yes? What was his reaction?"

"He informed me that someday I would regret the things I'd said to him."

"Did you tell Jekyll about these words?"

"Of course. Until this experiment of his became more than theory, we had almost no secrets." She sighed. "Now it seems we have nothing *but* secrecy between us."

"Hmm," I murmured, losing myself in thought. I noticed her crestfallen expression and put aside my deductions for the moment. "I do wish I had some words of comfort to give, but I simply have not yet learned enough of Henry Jekyll, and I have no wish to give false hope. I can tell he's a complicated man and that this experiment may very well mean more to him than anything else in his life." Then, because she had to be informed of the possibility, I said, "Including you."

Emma sighed. "You're not informing me of

anything I don't already know. In fact, I recently said as much to my father. My father . . . Oh, dear, what time is it?"

I pulled out my pocket watch. "A quarter to four."

"Oh, dear," she said again. "I must go. My father expects me tonight, I'm to play hostess for a business dinner."

"Then let us say good day, and I will see you to the door."

Emma stood, but as I attempted to get to my feet, a sharp, stabbing pain traveled the length of my right leg. Foolishly, I dropped my cane as I grasped my thigh with both hands. Because I was off-balance already, I fell heavily on my left side, back into the chair.

"Mr. Holmes!" Emma cried. She rushed to me and knelt down, one hand reaching to retrieve my cane, the other placing itself on my left knee. "You're so pale. Are you all right? What has happened to you?"

I grimaced, the pain settling into a throb, yet lessening none. Forcing myself to breathe, I said through gritted teeth, "I'll be fine, Miss. Nothing more than an old wound that chooses to act up at inopportune times."

She still looked worried as she handed me my cane. I accepted it gratefully. "Thank you. I'm sorry to say I must bid you good day from here."

"I dread leaving you in this state. Should I get someone to assist you?"

"No, no, I assure you, I will be fine. I just need time."

"If you are absolutely sure . . ." she trailed off. I could tell she was sincerely uncomfortable leaving me without doing something to help.

I exhaled through still clenched teeth. Conceding slightly, I said, "If you would tell Mrs. Hudson on your way out, I would be most grateful."

"That is all I can do?"

"Yes. But she will do what she can."

Nodding quickly, she backed away, saying, "Good day, Mr. Holmes. I do hope your leg is better soon." She got to her feet and exited the room.

I readjusted myself in the chair and immediately regretted it as another jolt of pain shot through my leg. Minutes later, I heard Mrs. Hudson's footfalls on the stairs. She knocked softly on the door and entered. "Mr. Holmes?"

"I'm sorry to bother you, Mrs. Hudson. Miss Carew didn't feel comfortable leaving without doing something in an effort to aid me. I have no choice but to wait for Watson to come back. He has an effective painkiller I've taken before."

"Are you sure there's nothing I can do?"

"Unfortunately, no."

She nodded and quietly backed out of the room and shut the door. As soon as it clicked closed, I found myself breathing shallowly, quickly, in a pointless attempt to relieve myself of some of the pain I hid while speaking with her. Watson had better return soon, I thought to myself. The initial mix he'd given me at the opera house did not take away all of the pain, but it brought things back to a manageable level. I sighed as I carefully massaged my thigh with the knuckles of my right hand, once again cursing Moriarty and his henchman. Cursing the fact that he'd disappeared, cursing that I'd found no trace of him since that November night, cursing my enduring plight that I do not have the true freedom to come and go from 221B when and why I need to.

Watson had warned me that there was a chance my leg's condition could deteriorate further, but I honestly didn't expect it would come to pass. I fenced with Erik in Paris! One would think if I could manage that feat, I could manage walking across a room!

Letting out another deep sigh, I took my pipe from the table next to my armchair and lit it. Taking only minimal comfort from the cloud of smoke that soon descended over me, I sunk lower in the seat, wincing, and silently waited for Watson's and Erik's respective returns.

*****

I awoke to the sound of a violin. Smiling in spite of the nagging pain in my leg, I opened my eyes to see Erik before me, my violin in his masterful hands.

"Ah, you're awake. Drink this."

Warily, I accepted the glass which held a clear liquid speckled with a rainbow assortment of floating flecks. "Is it quite safe?"

"It is a concoction I created in Paris."

That did not answer my question. "Is it quite safe?"

He smiled. "It will do you no harm."

Holding my breath, I gulped it down in one swallow. A sudden warmth spread through my entire body and then centered itself in my leg, making what felt like a cocoon around the muscles. Surprisingly, the pain lessened, and minutes later, had dissipated to almost nothing.

"If I didn't know better, I'd say you created a magic potion."

He laughed. "No, no magic, Holmes. Pure and simple herbs from the Orient, carefully mixed and administered."

"My leg feels marvelously better, in any case."

"I'm glad. Do not try to move too much for at least three quarters of an hour, though. The 'potion,' if you will, needs time to absorb into your system."

"I have no objection to remaining still."

"I'd hoped my playing would soothe you as you slept, but not even my skills could erase the pain from your face." He set the violin down and pulled up a chair next to me. "What happened?"

Sighing, I explained, "You already know the circumstances I faced with the initial injury to my leg. Watson has remained vigilante about examinations, looking over the muscle, the bone, testing my flexibility and such. After one of those times, he explained to me that he was worried about atrophy setting in, especially during my darker periods, where I'm likely not to move for extended periods of time. He told me it was possible my leg could get worse."

"Do you believe this is a sign?"

"Possibly. I already got proof of Watson's accuracy when we came back from the opera house. I thought I had failed you. That you would let yourself die in your lair after losing Christine. I'm afraid I came back here and fell into a rather deep depression. I barely moved for weeks, if not longer. The morning I got your letter, I went to stand, and was wracked with horrible pains throughout not only my leg, but the entire right side of my body. I called for Mrs. Hudson and she and I were able to manage the pain with hot, wet cloths and massage. It had mostly gone away after a few hours and I was stable enough to move around, carefully, and to play my violin while standing. My weight centered over my left leg, of course."

"Of course," Erik agreed.

"When Watson came later that day, I told him of your letter, we talked about a few mundane subjects, and then I told him what I had experienced that morning. He insisted on a thorough examination right there and came to the conclusion that I mustn't let myself be so stagnant in my movements again. I must give my leg at least some kind of easy exercise each day. I've kept to that, even in my darker moods, because I never wanted to experience that degree of pain again. And I haven't, until today. Erik, I . . ." My cold, calculated way of conveying the story failed me as I looked him in the eyes. "I could not even stand."

Erik was silent for a long moment. Then, "Let us see if you can now."

"It hasn't been three quarters of an hour."

"Let us see," he repeated. "I'm not asking you to dance. Only stand." He stood and extended his hand to me.

"Is your concoction that potent?" I asked. He just held his hand out expectantly. Leaving my cane next to the chair, I grasped his hand and let him pull me gently to my feet. Once there, he let me lean on his shoulder while I tested my right leg.

"It does seem to be a miraculous potion," I said, reaching for my cane and taking a few careful steps with its assistance.

"Easy, Holmes."

"I'm aware. I shall rest."

"Good. We'll all need to be at our best to help Jekyll."

Though my back was to him so he couldn't see, my face immediately fell. "I shall never be at my best again," I murmured.

Erik approached and put a hand on my shoulder. I heard a rustle and a low snap and Erik's hand guided me to turn and face him. When I did, I saw he had removed his mask, revealing his ruined face for me to see more closely than I ever had before.

"And I shall never attract a woman with my boyish good looks," he said, a hint of sarcasm in his voice and a grim smile on his twisted lips. "But you told me, and have shown me, that it doesn't matter. It's a horribly overused cliché, and I never thought I would be spouting this particular one, but it truly is what's inside that counts."

I gave a self-mocking smile. "And what do I have inside that would be of use to anyone? That truly matters to anyone?"

"Holmes, do not tell me you genuinely need this question answered."

I smiled in self-pity. "Even I have the unfortunate ability to lose confidence. Watson's writings never paint me in that light."

"Very well. You possess the courage to continue solving cases even in the face of judgment because of your leg. A cunning, brilliant mind that lets you out-think nearly any opponent. And despite how coldly logical and analytical you can be, you care about those around you.

Do you really think I'd be here, alive today, if these weren't qualities present in your personality?"

I stared at him, wanting to respond, but for once, I was at a loss as to what to say. I had my own tragedies in my past, but I was not so vain to think my own outnumbered Erik's. His admission that I had, in what I'd felt was an extremely inadequate way, saved his life brought something of a sense of peace to me. For the first time in my life, when that oppressive cloud of melancholia threatened to engulf me, I was asking for help. From none other than Erik. I did not even trust Watson this much. And Erik responded in kind, baring his heart to me and letting me know what he saw in me.

With these realizations, I found I felt strangely better. The cloud dispersed without consuming me. "Thank you, Erik."

"You're welcome, Holmes."

Our eyes met and mutual understanding flashed between us. No thanks were truly needed; I'd been there for him, so it was only right for him to reciprocate, to his way of thinking. Yet it was not duty or responsibility he felt obliged to fulfill. It was simply a matter of who he was. Who we both were.

Suddenly, I realized I had been expecting Watson to come to Baker Street as well. "Has Watson contacted you? I thought he'd be here by now, as well."

"Yes, he caught me before I came back here. He said he was sorry, but his wife needs him. A relative of his wife's was injured and Mrs. Watson is understandably upset and worried. Watson went with her to look after the relative."

"That will take precedence over Watson's

company with us for several days, I'm sure. Regrettable, but he should be with his wife. And after all, medicine is his career practice. We must move forward with this case without him."

"What did you learn when you talked to Jekyll?"

"He used an odd word when he did speak of the experiment."

"Oh?"

"He said 'volunteer.' I must admit, this leads me to believe the idea of Simon Stride being the victim may very well be a dead end."

"Unless he deliberately chose that word to throw off your suspicion," Erik suggested.

"No, there wasn't the slightest hesitation in his voice as he answered. He was giving a truthful answer, which leads me to once again think it is his father, and whatever Jekyll is doing, I feel it's failing."

"Why is that?"

"He told me, and I quote, 'No one can help me.'"

Erik considered this for a long moment. "Perhaps Jekyll believes he is the only one capable of saving his father. Jekyll could have convinced himself that his father's non-responsiveness makes him a willing volunteer."

"Assuming the father is the one being experimented on, that is exactly the conclusion I reached."

Nodding in agreement, Erik suggested sitting once again, and then said, "You also dabble -- more than dabble -- in chemistry matters. Why should Jekyll not ask for your assistance?"

I looked at him, hard, as I lowered myself onto the couch. "Erik, would you have asked for someone's assistance in the opera house?"

He opened his mouth. Shut it a moment later. "Touché, Holmes."

Just to punctuate my point, I continued. "Henry Jekyll was ridiculed for years by a Board of supposed professionals. He will not risk asking for help when the one he is experimenting on is having it done -- for all intents and purposes -- illegally." I sat back down. "I'm famished. Shall we ask Mrs. Hudson to bring us some dinner?"

"Already done while you were asleep. She should be up in --" he stopped as we both heard her footfalls on the stairs.

A moment later, she backed in the door, carrying a large silver tray. Erik cleared a spot on my chemistry table, then turned to give her some assistance. However, both of us had forgotten he had not put his mask back on, so when Mrs. Hudson turned and saw him, she let out a frightful shriek and very nearly dropped the tray.

Very quickly and brilliantly composing herself, she said, with barely a quiver in her voice, "Oh, Monsieur Erik, you really must not delight in frightening me so! Especially not when I'm holding your dinner tray." She smiled and set the tray down, then left the room.

Erik replaced his mask and glanced at me quizzically. "Did she just act like I'd done that for the purpose of scaring her for fun?"

I could hardly hold back a smile. ""Indeed, she did."

"Remarkable woman, that Mrs. Hudson."
"Yes, she is."

Chapter Five - Murder, Murder!

The morning of the twenty-sixth, Watson burst into 221B, startling Erik and me.

"Holmes, Erik! Sir Danvers has been murdered!"

Erik leaped to his feet and I sat up straighter in my chair, saying, "Murdered? Come, sit down. Tell us everything you know."

As he took a seat on the couch, I could tell Watson was thoroughly shaken by his knowledge. His countenance was pale and fine tremors ran up and down his arms, making his fingers tremble against his knees.

"I was awakened very early this morning to frenzied knocking at my door. It was an inspector, the one who had been called to the scene. He wished for my input in an examination and autopsy of the body. As we hurried to the mortuary, he explained that the normal physician who does this was out of town, and someone suggested me since they knew I was nearby, caring for my wife's cousin." He stopped, taking a deep breath.

"Are you sure you're quite well enough to repeat this?" Erik asked him.

"Yes," he forced out. "Yes, I have to be. For it -- whether directly or indirectly, I don't know -- ensnares Jekyll."

"Jekyll? What do you mean? Speak quickly now, Watson!" I instructed.

"A maid witnessed the murder last night. She was two houses down and saw it from a second-story window. Sir Danvers was walking away from the house she was in, on the same side of the street. She said it was almost midnight and, from a distance, a second man approached from the opposite side of the street. Apparently, Sir Danvers appeared to recognize the second man and raised his hand in greeting. The other saw him and stopped. When Sir Danvers walked over, the maid saw the second fellow push back the cloak he had around his shoulders and pull out a thick wooden cane. He bludgeoned Sir Danvers repeatedly, and so violently that when he was done, the cane was in two pieces. He left the body where it fell and threw the one half of the cane away."

"The police found the cane, I assume?" I asked.

"Yes. Well, half of it. It was with the body when I got there to examine it. And this is what ties Jekyll in. Holmes, the cane was his."

"His? Of course, it was the one he received for his accomplishments, correct?"

"Yes, exactly. One of the policemen I spoke to said he remembered being at the ceremony."

"Yes, I have notes about his procurement of the instrument in my file."

"Might I see it?" Watson asked.

"Of course." I told him where he could find the thin file and Watson found it, quickly scanning the words. "Yes, the initials of recognition are the very same."

"I suppose there is no chance the cane was stolen from Jekyll's residence," Erik said.

"That was the inspector's speculation. I was questioned briefly when I was with them. It seems only the three of us have entered Jekyll's house aside from Sir Danvers, Miss Emma, Utterson, and Poole in almost a month."

"Indeed? Are we needed for questioning, then?" I

asked.

"I'm uncertain. The police seemed satisfied with my answers, but they may call on you. Nothing was reported by anyone else about the house being burgled."

"Hmm . . . this poses two possibilities, then. Either the man in question--"

"Holmes? Why did you stop?" Watson asked.

"This maid. Did she get a description of the attacker? Anything distinguishing about his person?"

"Unfortunately, no. All the maid could see was that he was wearing a black cloak, black trousers, and black boots, and a black top hat with a white stripe. She thought he had longer hair, but couldn't be sure; it could have been a shadow across his face."

"Nothing definitive about his gait?"

"That was the odd thing. The maid mentioned there seemed to be some kind of deformity or malformation about him, though she couldn't pinpoint specifically what it was."

I rubbed my chin thoughtfully. "Then there are three possibilities. This man is either a friend or colleague of Jekyll's. Someone to whom he would entrust a possession. Or he is someone with information with which to blackmail Jekyll. Perhaps he's become aware of intimate details of the experiment and that is why Jekyll spoke nothing of a stolen possession. Lastly, this man wants to discredit or frame Jekyll and did not foresee a witness coming forth."

"Stride," Erik said. "What better way to attempt to utterly destroy Jekyll than by murdering his fiancée's father? Not only that, but if Jekyll was successfully framed and therefore removed, Stride could swoop in to claim Emma."

"Likely," I said, steepling my fingers in front of my face, my elbows on the arms of the chair. "We must find out if Stride has an alibi for last night. He did threaten Jekyll and told Miss Emma that she would regret rejecting him."

"I think visiting Jekyll would be a wise idea," Watson said. "But if he's heard about this, I doubt he will admit anyone to his quarters. I was told the man was like a father to him, and Sir Danvers himself told me he viewed Jekyll as a son."

"Leave Jekyll to me. I'll confront him somehow. Erik, can you find Stride? I believe of the three of us, you will succeed in intimidating him the most."

Erik gave a wicked smile beneath the mask and went to the door. "I'll return in an hour. I'll also find out what I can about gaining entrance to Jekyll's house."

"Thank you."

Watson watched Erik leave, then turned back to me, a look of incredulity on his face.

"Yes, Watson?" I said, stifling a laugh. He looked quite ridiculous.

"Holmes . . . normally you would be the one intimidating Stride."

"Erik is more than sufficient to perform that duty."

"I don't doubt it, but Holmes, you are content to let him take the action?"

Sighing, I closed my eyes and said, "No, I'm not. But I feel I have no choice at the moment."

"Holmes, what are you speaking of?"

"On the afternoon of the twenty-second, I had another episode with my leg, much like the one I described to you that happened to me after coming out of the melancholia following the opera house case." I opened my eyes and looked at him.

Watson's eyes widened. "I'm so sorry, Holmes. Are you all right? I apologize for not being here to help."

"Please don't. You needed to be with your wife. Your practice and your wife's family are important as well. Erik gave me a concoction of his own making and it took the pain away very effectively. However, I promised him I would rest my leg so it potentially won't happen again for a long while. I only agreed because . . ."

"Because . . . ? Holmes, because what?"

Closing my eyes again, I rested my forehead on my fingertips and said, "Because I'm afraid of being fully crippled."

Watson, blissfully, said nothing, merely putting a reassuring hand on my shoulder.

*****

When Erik returned, he assured us that Stride had an alibi for the time Sir Danvers was murdered. He'd checked with the constables, who were also aware of Stride's threat and had already interrogated the man.

"The alibi holds. Stride was on a train coming back from visiting relatives."

"How long has he been away?"

"Over a week now."

"Which means that he can't be Jekyll's victim," Watson said.

"Yes, I'd already nearly thrown out that possibility because of Jekyll's words. It's good we now have confirmation."

"'"Which brings us back to it being the father," Erik said.

"Indeed, it does," I agreed. "Were you able to learn anything about Jekyll?"

"He has locked himself in his lab and will see no one, not even Poole or Utterson. I knelt down by that boarded-up window again, and I could hear Jekyll crying within, repeatedly sobbing 'why?'"

"We shall not attempt to see him for a day or two. However, we mustn't wait too long. In his state of grief, he may, if pressed, give something away." I pulled out my pipe, simply running my fingers over the smooth wooden surface. "I will go there tomorrow. This time, Jekyll *will* answer to me."

Chapter Six - Sympathy, Tenderness

September 27th, 1:00 pm

The police have just left my residence. Sir Danvers Carew has been murdered. Oh, dear God, what have I done? I have unleashed this beast on the world. He is terrible, horrible, deplorable, despicable in every sense of the words, yet . . . I find I cannot hate him. I abhor his actions and I must admit, he is truly the most hateful being I've had any sort of association with, but . . . I disturbingly find myself having a father's interest in his actions. Except for this latest regrettable one. However, I've delighted myself in observing his nature, his habits, his decisions in carving out a place for himself in this world.

Yet in a perverse fashion, he has a son's indifference towards me. Indifference and something of a spiteful attitude no matter how kindly a suggestion is given. Though perhaps that is because kindness is not something he seems to understand. He is so full of malice. It's like a poison that has infected his veins, distorting every aspect of him. I know things cannot continue as they are. Things are going too far in a direction I did not foresee. I must regain control of the situation.

The police questioned me about Sir Danvers's murder because a walking stick was found near his body. Not just any walking stick! Mine, the one I received years ago, meant to honor me as a doctor and scientist. What would all of my colleagues think of me now, I wonder? What would they think if they knew I lied to the police? That I am indeed intimately familiar with the man they seek? I wonder if, as his appearance does for me, his name would provide as much disgust and alarm?

The name Edward Hyde . . .

Sherlock Holmes

Despite the ever-nagging fear that my leg could give out on me again, and the discomfort I suffered to walk long distances, I trudged my way to the Jekyll household on September twenty-seventh, starting out shortly after two in the afternoon. I simply wanted to take the time to think, because I sincerely had no idea how I would bypass Poole and actually talk to Jekyll if indeed he had concealed himself in his laboratory and refused to see even his closest companions. Despite my assurances to Watson that breaking and entering was something I would not do, I'd considered the notion. Yet I was aware that such an action was not something to be taken lightly, and only to be used as an absolute last resort.

I was so lost in thought that I didn't hear the young lady trying to get my attention until she roughly grabbed my arm and stopped right in front of me. Yanked from my stupor, I focused on her annoyed expression and the tightness of her fingers on my bicep.

"I know you upper class folk like t' pretend people such as me don't exist durin' daylight hours," she started angrily, "but I need some 'elp. I'm not lookin' t' offer you my services."

She was the prostitute, Lucy, from the Red Rat. But of course, she wouldn't recognize me; I was in disguise the last time I saw her.

"My name is Sherlock Holmes," I said slowly, pointedly glancing at her hand until she released her hold. She didn't step back, though, and her eyes still flashed angrily. "I assure you, I wasn't ignoring you based on any degree of social status. I was lost in thought over a case I'm investigating. I'm a consulting detective by profession, you see. May I be of some assistance?"

"Maybe you can 'elp me detect where in this city 'arley Street is, then, if you're that good at findin' things," she said. Then she peered at me. "You *are* good at what you do, right?"

"Indeed, madam, I am." Wait a moment. Harley Street? That was where Jekyll resided. "Why are you trying to find Harley Street?"

"I'm lookin' for 'im," she said, holding out a business card to me. Indeed, it was Jekyll's. I grinned slightly. "I've never been t' this part of the city, y'see, so I don't know where the street is. But I have t' find it."

"Are you ill in some way?" I asked, deciding to play along and see how much her words would reveal.

"Not ill, sir, but 'urt. Y'see, I'm . . . well, you prob'ly already detected what I am. Polite folk like you would say I'm an unfortunate. Or a lady of the night, if you catch my drift."

"Yes, I do indeed. And yes, I had already discerned your profession."

"Profession, 'ah!" she gave a sarcastic laugh. "That's a interestin' way t' put it. It's not like I chose it, you understand. But when a girl gets down on 'er luck, she's gotta do what she can to keep bread in 'er stomach, ain't she?"

I nodded, staring at the card again. I already knew from the roundabout way we'd spoken before, that she was no accomplice of Jekyll's. I'd dismissed her after that, deducing that she was of no major importance to the case. But suddenly I found myself wondering why she had Jekyll's card. It was, of course, something she wouldn't mention possessing to a stranger. Especially not one so bedraggled as I had appeared. Why *did* he give it to her? Did he perhaps have a darker interest in the London nightlife? Was his relationship and upcoming marriage with Miss Emma Carew not enough to satisfy his more base urges?

Perhaps he derived some intellectual stimulation from this girl, because she did seem to be more than the two dimensional prostitute only out for the money men would give in return for sexual favors so the woman in question could buy food, lodgings, or cheap alcohol.

"Please, go on. You said you were hurt?" I asked.

"Yes. Well, a gent came by two nights ago, 'round nine, I s'pose. Bought me for th' evenin'. I was 'appy 'bout that. Not what I'd 'ave to do, but the money 'e'd claimed 'e'd give me. It would've been enough, I coulda kept off the street for a week, maybe more. Most men like it when I take control. Make th' rules, as it were. But 'im, 'e pushed me down on th' bed, 'ad 'is way with me, and turned me on my stomach an' cut up my back real 'ard. I was so 'urt, I could barely move. I tried to get up when 'e demanded me to. 'E was yellin' at me and throwin' things and everythin' else, but I couldn't! I was 'urt and bleedin' too much. So 'e got even angrier and left me where I was and went out on th' streets."

I was horrified. Horrified enough that I forgot her station and the way the constables of this city would view her. "What a terrible ordeal. But why have you waited in searching for assistance? And have you gone to the police?"

She gave a cruel laugh. "A girl like me, tellin' the

74

coppers about a guy like 'im? 'E may have looked odd, but 'e's a rich gent, and--"

"Looked odd?" I interrupted. "How do you mean?"

"Well . . ." She thought for a long moment, scrunching up her nose in concentration. "'E was sort of . . . shriveled-lookin'. Like 'is clothes was too big for 'im. And 'e walked kinda funny. Almost like there was somethin' wrong with 'im, but I don't know what."

"Why not?" I asked.

She gave me an indignant stare. "It's not like I'm a doctor, y'know. I really couldn't say. It wasn't anythin' definite, just somethin' y'got the feelin' of, if you know what I mean?"

"Yes, I believe I do," I said. Whoever this man was, it was almost certainly the same one who killed Sir Danvers. "Let us hurry to Harley Street."

When we arrived on Jekyll's doorstep, Poole hesitantly let us in, and only because Lucy insistently showed him Jekyll's card. Poole left us in the parlor, a room I felt I was becoming altogether too intimately acquainted with, and went to fetch Jekyll.

I merely observed Lucy as her mouth dropped open at the sight of such opulence. She stared in amazement at nearly every nook and cranny and then turned to me, a huge smile on her face.

"This is a marvelous place, isn't it, Mr. Sherlock 'olmes?"

"Yes. Yes, it is," I agreed quietly. An unreasonable sadness that I did not allow to show on my face assailed me as I considered the childlike wonder present in this woman. She must have had all her other dreams fail her, or perhaps the social status into which she was born was not favorable to a wide range of professions.

"Miss?" Poole said moments later, reappearing in the doorway. "Mr. Jekyll will see you in but a moment."

Lucy smiled and gave a quick curtsey. Poole eyed me suspiciously, but said nothing as he vacated the doorway.

Soon enough, Jekyll walked in. He stopped abruptly when he saw me, but then his eyes found Lucy. She stepped towards him, oblivious of his discomfort with my presence, and said, "'Ello. D'you remember me?"

"Um . . ." His mind obviously on other things, he nonetheless searched her face, looking for any hint of familiarity. He blinked several times, but no recognition lit up his eyes. "No, I'm sorry, Miss, I don't."

"It's *Lucy*." When he didn't respond, she put her hands on her hips. "Lucy 'arris? The girl from that night . . . You gave me your card. For if I ever needed a friend?"

"Oh, oh, yes!" Jekyll said, focusing on the card she held up. "Yes, I do recall saying if you ever needed . . ."

"A friend," Lucy continued. "And I do. I was just telling Mr. 'olmes about it. I was attacked by a 'customer' of mine two nights ago."

"Attacked? Two nights?" That spurred Jekyll into alertness. "What happened?"

Instead of speaking, Lucy sat down on an ottoman near Jekyll, her back to him. She unbuttoned her blouse, shrugged it off her shoulders, and winced, hissing in a breath as the muscles and skin shifted with her sharp movement.

Jekyll's eyes widened. "Dear God," he breathed.

"What horrible wounds! Who--who did this to you?"

"A real English gentleman," she said sarcastically.

"Please, tell me about it," Jekyll requested as he got gauze, assorted ointments, a clean cloth, and cotton balls from his doctor's bag and poured antiseptic on a cloth. He gently pulled the material of her blouse aside a bit more to inspect the degree of damage to her skin.

Lucy looked to the intricate patterns of the carpet; it was obvious the idea of relating her nightly activities in front of Jekyll would be humiliating. A concept I found interesting and rather telling. Ladies of the night are not usually shy in their exploits with men. Once again, it struck me that she was not a usual unfortunate. She did not eye the items in the house with thinly-veiled greed, for one thing. Instead, there was honest interest. Not to mention that when one looked beyond the dialect she spoke with and met her eyes, there was an unmistakable shine of intelligence.

This was not some cheap and tawdry whore. This was an intelligent, thoughtful young woman whom life had been particularly cruel to.

All at once, it occurred to me that this was why Jekyll had given her his card if she ever needed a friend. He'd seen much the same in her that I just had. He'd given her something so few prostitutes ever receive: respect. She must have known that and now wished to show him respect in return, through her discretion.

Jekyll seemed distracted enough to not notice she wasn't speaking. He splashed more antiseptic on his cloth and warned, "This may sting."

"Don't worry, I'm used t'--" Her voice failed her as Jekyll touched the cloth to her skin. She hissed in another breath and clutched the skirt she was wearing with both hands until her knuckles were white. Jekyll put a reassuring hand on her shoulder.

As he cared for her wounds, Lucy relaxed somewhat and gave him vague details of the events she'd outlined for me.

"How horrible," Jekyll murmured, though it was obvious to me he was simply spouting platitudes at appropriate times. I also noted he did not suggest, as I had, that she alert the police.

As he finished with the cloth and began applying fresh, clean gauze to soothe and cover her injuries, Lucy happened to say, "Well, at least I know 'is name so's to warn the rest of the girls about 'im. Not a name I've heard before, but I'll not soon forget it, neither."

"And what was that?" Jekyll asked absently, cutting a piece of medical tape and applying it.

I leaned forward eagerly to catch what she said. She half-turned to look at him and, with none of the poorer section's dialect of dropping H's at the start of words, enunciated slowly, "Hyde. Edward Hyde."

I was not allowed even seconds of victory over learning Carew's murderer's name, because as soon as Lucy said it, Jekyll's hand slipped off her shoulder, and he paled and stumbled away from her. "Wh-what did you say?"

"Edward Hyde." She fully turned to face him. "What's wrong?"

"Noth--nothing. Nothing at all," he said as he straightened, though I could tell there was a struggle for control happening beneath the surface. "There is a perfectly competent doctor at number two Devonshire.

78

It's nearby. Why not go to him? Why . . . why come to me?"

"You gave me your card," she reminded.

"Yes, yes, I understand. But surely there is someone else to help you . . ."

Lucy, angry, brought her blouse back up and began buttoning it. "Someone else to 'elp me? No, there isn't. You gave me your card. Said if I ever needed a friend . . . But I guess it turns out I'm too low-class for you, eh? Well, I won't make that mistake again!"

She turned away from him and I could see her eyes were full of tears. I turned a cold eye on Jekyll who, I was surprised to see, looked downright tortured. Lucy escaped the room and I made a split-second decision to follow her. I only caught her at the door because the lock mechanism gave her trouble.

"Lucy," I said gently. "I don't believe he means to hurt you, or that you are too low-class for the likes of his 'lofty social position.'"

"Oh, no?" she asked, tears starting to course down her cheeks. "Then why isn't 'e 'ere, tellin' me this instead of you?"

"Henry Jekyll is . . ." I attempted to think of a way to describe this delicately, yet vaguely, "very consumed with his work at the present time. He's just recently gone through a personal tragedy. It's not that he cares nothing for you, or the danger you find yourself in."

"What *is* it then?" she asked emphatically. "Ever since I first met 'im, when 'e turned down my advances but said if I ever needed a friend, I've found myself . . . Well, you'll prob'ly think it's ridiculous for someone like me t' feel this way, but . . ." she trailed off, looking towards the room from which she had fled.

"You have feelings for him," I surmised in a low voice.

"Yes," she said, clearly surprised.

"Do not look so surprised. Just because I am primarily a coldly impartial logician does not mean I cannot recognize the feelings of a woman," I said.

Lucy gave a self-conscious grin, casting her eyes down. "Bein' 'ere, talkin' to you, well, it almost makes me feel like I'm a real lady."

I opened my mouth to reply when Jekyll, silhouetted in the far doorway, said, "You *are* a real lady."

She turned to him with wide, surprised, and pleased eyes. "You really think I am?"

"I do. I apologize for my behavior. But I can assure you, my social position has no bearing on how I see you. I'm something of an outcast in my own 'social circle,' anyway." He came up to her, took Lucy's hand and kissed it, then continued. "I'll remember you next time, should you decide to honor me again with your presence. I hope that you will warn your friends about . . . Hyde . . . and that you never have contact with him again." He paused, seeming to want to say much more, but settled on, "Should you ever see him again, run. I beg you, run."

Lucy nodded solemnly at his somber tone. "Well, I won't take up any more of your time." She curtsied. "Thank you for your 'elp. It's good to know there're really nice men out there."

Jekyll gave what seemed to be a self-derisive grunt and turned away, walking back to the room where he'd treated her. I opened the door for her, then closed it and followed Jekyll. He stood at the large fireplace, leaning against the mantel, his head on his arm. I approached him slowly, stopping about three feet away.

"Who is Edward Hyde?"

He jerked back and looked at me and for the first time, I saw how much more haggard and run-down his appearance was. His eyes, which had simply seemed nervous when last I saw him, now had the unmistakable tinge of insanity. "Henry," I said gently, "please. Tell me. Who is Edward Hyde?"

"He is . . . a colleague of mine."

There was only a slight pause in his sentence, but enough of one to tell me Jekyll had lied.

"A colleague. Close enough to borrow one of your possessions?"

"What? No, I wouldn't say that. He does not borrow my things."

"Oh, no? Then how did he have a cane of yours two nights ago?"

Jekyll met my unflinching eyes then, his own filled with fear and dread. "You believe Hyde killed Sir Danvers."

"Yes, I do. I think his evening with Lucy left him angry because it did not go as he planned. It was observed at first that Sir Danvers appeared to recognize the man who killed him. I think he mistook this Hyde character for someone else and because Hyde was already angry, he took that ferocity out on Sir Danvers. Not only that, he did it with your cane, Jekyll."

Jekyll looked away.

"Are you protecting a murderer?!" I demanded, leaning my weight on my left foot and picking up my own cane, brandishing it harmlessly in front of him. "Jekyll, *are you?"*

"No!" he shouted. "No, I could never protect such a deplorable, despicable being! Sometimes I hardly think he's human!"

Resting my cane back on the floor, I said, "So you do have more familiarity with him than merely being colleagues."

He sighed. "Yes. Yes, I do. I cannot explain how, though, and to that decision, I remain adamant. You will not change my mind with either kindness or threats."

"I plan to attempt neither," I assured him. "I believe you when you say you aren't protecting him. But . . . one last question: how long have you known Hyde?"

"Oh . . ." Jekyll gave it some careful thought. "I suppose it could be said I've been aware of him for as long as I can remember. But we've only become so . . . intimately acquainted . . . in the past few weeks."

"Hmm. Interesting. Thank you, Henry."

He looked at me sharply. "You act as though I've given something away."

"Do I? I apologize. No, you've given nothing away. Merely given me food for thought."

Jekyll gave me another sharp glance. After learning about my methods, and then testing them on me, I had no doubt he understood that I had lied. How much he guessed I knew, though, was another matter. In the end, he turned and walked away, muttering to himself as he went. I caught the term 'HJ-7,' but had no context with which to hypothesize what that could be.

Food for thought, indeed. A plan began to form in my mind, but I would need Erik's assistance to truly succeed.

From the Journal of John H. Watson, M.D.

Holmes caned his way up the stairs and into 221B, nearly collapsing as he opened the door. Erik and I immediately went to his aid, supporting him as he limped to his chair. Once he was seated, he thanked us, took his pipe out, and lit it.

"Holmes, I thought you were going to stay off your leg? Not do so much walking around," I said.

"Indeed, I had decided that, but I felt the walk would help me mentally, though it has definitely hampered me physically." He looked at Erik. "I do apologize for not taking better note of your instructions, but remaining in a near constant state of carefully planned stillness and only light exercise is something I shall never get used to, I'm afraid."

"You must learn your limits, Holmes. And by God, at least take a hansom cab on the return trip!" Erik said in a sarcastically good-natured tone.

"Dually noted," Holmes said. He went on to speak of seeing Lucy, what transpired at Jekyll's, and then told us he had a new theory about the experiment.

"What is it, Holmes?" I asked.

"Henry said he's been aware of Hyde almost as far back as his memory stretches, but has only become so closely entwined with him in the *last few weeks.*"

"*Hyde* is the subject of the experiment?" I asked, shocked not only at the idea, but that I had spoken before Erik.

"It could very well be. Hyde has been described by two different people as having some kind of deformity, or appearing to, but neither was able to pinpoint *what,* specifically."

"You think the experiment could affect a person physically?" Erik asked.

"Possibly. When someone isn't born with a deformity, it can be difficult for others to pinpoint exactly what is wrong."

"I wouldn't know," Erik said darkly.

"But I believe Hyde would," Holmes said. "Now, the question emerges, how do we find him? And Erik, I'm afraid you and I have a mission tomorrow."

"Yes?"

"Though I hesitate to do so while he is obviously home so often, I must take the risk and gain entrance to Jekyll's laboratory."

"Holmes, no!" I exclaimed. "What if Jekyll is in there? What if you're caught? I know that you have some sway with the inspectors of the city, but even they cannot turn a blind eye if you are caught trespassing." Another thought occurred to me, and for some reason, this struck me as even more horrible than Holmes being arrested. "Holmes, what if *Hyde* is in there?"

"Indeed. All of these things have crossed my mind as well. It's part of the reason I didn't take a cab back. I wanted time and solitude to think over my options, as well as each one of those possibilities. After all, Hyde has already killed one man --" he stopped when he saw me pale and Erik's jaw clench. "I'm sorry. Yes, Hyde's description fits that of the man who killed Carew. Nonetheless, I must take the chance."

"In addition," Erik said before I could open my mouth to protest, "I've killed before as well. I shall bring my Punjab lasso. For protection only, I give my word. However, should we chance to cross paths with Hyde, I will not hesitate to use it, simply to render him harmless."

"Agreed, as long as you don't raise your own death count by one," Holmes said. He massaged his leg. "Perhaps I should have thought more carefully about this excursion. Erik, do you have anymore of that wonderful concoction?"

I looked at Erik who seemed to produce a vial of clear liquid with an assortment of colored specks out of thin air. He handed it to Holmes and Holmes swallowed it in one quick gulp.

"Thank you," Holmes said, handing back the vial. "Oh, that *is* extremely bitter."

Erik took it, merely nodding his acknowledgement. "It can be taken as you just have, but it's much more pleasing to the palate when mixed in something hot, like tea."

Holmes smacked his lips several times, no doubt trying to rid himself of the taste, and I took my chance to ask, "I suppose I have no chance of convincing you not to enter Jekyll's laboratory?"

"I'm sorry, Watson, but no. We know he has a journal. If that has nothing on the experiment in it, he must have notes, *something* that will shed more light on what his hope is, or who his 'volunteer' is. Once I find that, things will connect much more easily. I should like to get the information from Jekyll himself, but that will not happen. Whatever he's doing, he's determined to do it alone."

As I was about to open my mouth, an idea occurred to me. A way I could assist Holmes and occupy

Jekyll so that Holmes could, God willing, find what he was searching for. To Holmes's and Erik's surprise, I got to my feet and, quickly excusing myself, left the room.

I had to find Utterson.

Chapter Seven - I Need To Know

"Do you often make it a point to break into houses when your investigations have reached a dead end?" I asked Holmes when we were in the hansom cab on the way to Jekyll's.

"On the contrary, my friend, the investigation is not at a dead end. This is merely an interlude to get to the next step."

"I see you have expertly dodged answering my question."

"You, of all folks, are wary of trespassing to gain advancement in a case?" At my silence, Holmes gave a grin. "Why risk incriminating oneself?"

Minutes later, the hansom cab stopped down the street from Jekyll's house. Holmes paid the driver, but before we got out, I stopped him. "Holmes, look."

Henry Jekyll was running out of his house, away from where we were sitting, shrugging on a black overcoat at the same time.

"This is a marvelous bit of good fortune," I said, wondering if this truly was a coincidence.

"Yes," Holmes murmured, his tone giving away that he speculated the same thing.

We waited to exit the cab until Jekyll was well out of sight. Then, I led Holmes to the boarded-up window at the back of the house.

"Good, the bushes have been cut back. I can remove the wood easily enough, but it's so rotted through, it will never go back in place in one piece."

"I'm not worried about that. We'll do what we can

to replace it. I simply want to get into the laboratory."

Nodding, I knelt to the ground and carefully picked up and moved the wood. As I expected, it crumbled apart between my fingers, littering the grass on its way to where I deposited the partially intact larger piece.

"No glass in the window. Good," Holmes said. He lowered himself so he was sitting on the edge of the window frame. "Your assistance, please?"

I took his arms and he moved forward so that my hands were the only things keeping him from falling to the floor below.

"My feet can just touch the ground, Erik. Release me, then drop me my cane," he requested.

I grunted my agreement, let his hands go one at a time, and handed his cane down a moment later.

"Holmes, would you like me to come down as well?"

"No, I need you to remain alert for anyone who may come by." I heard papers rustling and then, "I believe I know what I'm searching for, anyway."

Minutes, that seemed like hours, later, Holmes said, "Yes, indeed! I've found what I'm looking for."

He appeared below me, tossed his cane up to me, and pocketed something too quickly for me to see. "Pull me back up," he appealed.

Once we were both back outside the house, he checked his pocket. "Good. Still safe."

"What did you take, Holmes?"

He shook his head, indicating we should leave the premises. When we were back in a hansom cab on our way back to Baker Street, Holmes said, "Henry muttered yesterday about something called HJ-7. I found a dozen vials, only eight of them labeled and filled with any amount of liquid, from HJ-1 to HJ-8. I've procured number seven."

"What will that do Holmes?"

"Perhaps nothing, possibly everything. This could be what he is administering to his patient. There was a needle nearby, so I assume he injects it directly into the bloodstream. Ah, we're back home."

The cab stopped in front of 221B and we paid the driver and left the cab. Once we were back in Holmes's rooms, he set himself up at his chemistry table.

"Erik, I know you would undoubtedly like to assist me, but I find right now, more than anything, I need music. Would you mind?"

"Of course not." I took Holmes's violin from its case and tuned it, then brought the bow over the strings. I lost myself minutes later in music I had learned over years of study. I played pieces of my own composition. When I could think of no other pieces, my fingers worked their way to new combinations of notes I hoped I could recall later.

As I let my fingers have free reign to create music, I found my mind began to wander. As unfortunate a creature as Jekyll seemed to be, I found I could relate to him. We both had someone we were desperate to save. However, whereas he looked inward to save another, I had looked to another to save myself.

I came slightly out of my reverie at that thought, recalling something Holmes had once hinted at. He'd warned me to halt my pursuit of Christine because to do otherwise would mean the complete destruction of my heart. He'd only ever hinted at the story behind this, but he'd said he understood loving a woman so profoundly. In fact, it had cost him his own heart. It was the real reason he was so calculating, so analytical. Because when he wasn't being that man, the Sherlock Holmes the world knew, he was a broken soul, defeated by the most illogical of all emotions: love.

I found I was envious of Holmes. Of the methodical, yet casual way he went about his work, no one ever guessing that a broken heart lay beneath the surface. Of course, I was just as good at the façade, but I doubted that would still be the case if I had to be around people day in and day out.

Holmes's voice broke into my thoughts. "Ah-ha!"

The bow made a loud screech as my playing came to a sudden standstill. "What have you found?"

"This is indeed a serum meant to go directly into the patient's bloodstream. To ingest it would be fatal. Jekyll has used some very rare, very potent chemicals in this mix. Interesting that through the blood, it's tolerable, yet over the tongue, deadly."

"What might it do to a person? Is there any way to find out its rate of tolerability through injection?"

"Through these experiments, doubtful."

"I became extremely familiar with poisons, herbs, and other potentially lethal things to ingest during my time in Persia. Whatever is in that vial could prove incredibly painful through injection. One poison I became aware of would be put on the tip of a dart, then blown into someone's flesh. When the poison entered the bloodstream, it caused incredible hallucinations--"

"Enough that the person was driven to their death," Holmes interrupted. "I was once involved in a case where an Egyptian cult used poisoned darts with hallucinogenic properties."

"Somehow I'm not surprised. But no, not driven to death. Recall that I was used by the khanum in *torture* devices. She didn't want the victims killed. The poison I spoke of would make the person feel like their skin was on fire. Or that their inner organs were melting. Of course, Jekyll wouldn't deliberately poison or torture a person, so we hope, but what if injecting this felt that way? It would......."

"--explain the screams," Holmes finished for me. "Indeed, it could. As for what it does . . ." He held the vial up in front of his narrowed eyes. "I'm unsure. I have an idea or two to find out, but those must wait. Especially taking into account the possibilities you presented, I'll have to run more tests before I attempt something that drastic."

"Drastic?" I didn't like the sound of that.

"Do not worry, Erik. There are many roads I can take before that one."

"I hope you'll explore all the others carefully, then," was all I said.

"I shall."

"Holmes?"

"Yes?"

"Would you permit me to inquire about your past a moment?"

He set the vial down in one of his holders and looked at me carefully. "That depends on what you wish to find."

I smiled. "It seems to me I once said something similar to you the first time you came to my lair."

"Yes, you did. Though I truly wasn't searching for something specific. I deduce the same cannot be said for you."

"You're correct."

"What *do* you wish to find?"

"Only the story behind why you have such an acute understanding of the destruction of the human heart."

A pained, haunted look crossed Holmes's face. "I'm sorry, Erik. Even this many years later, it is something I cannot speak of. It's just . . ." he turned away, his hand going up to his face, his knuckles on the other turning white as they gripped the table. "It's not something I can speak of," he repeated.

"Holmes . . ." For the first time in years, I was struck speechless. That catch in his voice, the fact that he turned away from me, the hand at his face . . . was Sherlock Holmes *crying?*

Putting down the violin, I went to stand next to him and rested my arm around his shoulders. "You don't have to say anything, Holmes. I'm sorry for bringing it up so abruptly. I apologize for asking at all."

He took in a sharp breath and swiped his hand across his eyes. "No," he said, turning back to his chemistry table, my arm falling back to my side, "I should face these emotions one day. But . . . after hiding from them or running from them for so long . . ."

"You don't know where to start," I completed.

"Yes. Exactly." He sighed deeply. "How I envy you at times."

"Envy me?" I asked in shock.

"Indeed. You believed me so quickly after the

conclusion with Christine when I told you that your life was worth living. It took me months to even consider that perhaps I could keep breathing. It was only about a year before I met Watson that I came to the conclusion that perhaps my life carried some meaning. You, I hint at my own experiences and despite your own heartbreak over Christine, you were not broken. You put faith in me. You were willing to trust, to whatever miniscule degree, that my words held grains of truth. I could not have done the same so quickly after the events in my past."

I had no words. All I could do was stand next to him a moment longer. Then, he went back to the vial and his microscopes and tests, and after a long moment, I moved back to pick up his violin and continue playing for him. Of course, I'd suspected this before, but this was the first time I was acutely aware of the duality within Sherlock Holmes. To the world, he was a methodical, calculating, logical genius. Alone in the dark, he was . . . God only knew. He admitted to being envious of me. That was a concept I couldn't wrap my head around. Somehow I knew he meant on a deeper level, but I couldn't get past the fact that he'd admitted to being envious of a masked musician who had kidnapped a singer and brought her down to his lair beneath the opera house in which she sang. Even on a deeper level, I was debatably insane, horribly tempered, prone to rash decisions . . .

I suppose it was all a matter of perception. All I knew about Holmes at that moment was that only one word could come close to the emotion I'd felt practically radiating off of him minutes ago: haunted.

Sherlock Holmes

I remember Erik asking me that question. Yes, haunted was a good choice of word. Haunted was exactly how I felt. Haunted by a ghost I hoped would never leave me, yet at the same time I wanted desperately to forget. Which was a cause of great distress for me, making me feel guilty and, in the end, as if I was being pulled in two different directions.

The destruction of my own heart . . . I must admit, I led Erik a bit astray. It wasn't just a woman who contributed to that. There was another . . . However, it is a story for another time. The only reason these insinuations toward it are included is because that conversation contributed to my coming decisions and how I ultimately handled things. I can't say things would have been different had my more negative emotions and memories not been closer to the surface. Indeed, they may very well have been worse, what with the more negative ones being repressed. I suppose I'll never know. Truth be told, I don't *want* to know.

Chapter Eight - Obsession

I'd fallen asleep at my chemistry table that night, so I had a very unpleasant experience waking up the following morning. Especially since I was jolted awake by the sharp rapping at the door.

"Who is it rapping, rapping on your chamber door?" I heard Erik mutter as he went to answer it.

I smiled at his reference to Poe's *The Raven,* but my mouth settled into a grim line when the door opened and an angry-looking Utterson stomped in.

"Mr. Holmes, Henry has asked that I come here and demand the return of what he believes you have stolen from his laboratory."

"Stolen? What do you speak of, Utterson? And why hurl the accusation at me?"

"Dr. Watson came to me and said the pharmacist who gives Henry has chemicals needed to speak with him personally. But when Henry got there, the pharmacist only gave him the chemicals, was paid, and said nothing he could not have said to me."

So that was where Watson went. He was making sure Jekyll would be away from the house so Erik and I would have uninterrupted time for our little excursion. From Utterson's words and expression, I could tell he was hard-pressed to believe I was capable of theft. Fortunate. This would only require a logical train of thought.

"Perhaps Watson simply misunderstood the situation. And honestly, Utterson, such circumstantial threads of 'evidence' like that should not make one so flippantly accuse a man. I'd say that it's much more likely that the man who murdered Sir Danvers gained illegal entry to Jekyll's laboratory and stole something."

Utterson visibly calmed. "Yes . . . I would say you're absolutely right. After all, Henry's cane was found on the scene."

I caned over to my chair and sat down. "Precisely. However, if Jekyll wishes to speak with me, I will gladly meet with him to dispel any doubts that he may have."

"If you would, Mr. Holmes. I would greatly appreciate it," he said, fully back to his formal, polite self.

"Of course. What time is it?" I pulled out my pocket watch and saw quarter after eight. "I shall come by later this afternoon, say around three, if you don't mind. My leg needs time to stretch and I'm afraid I fell asleep at my chemistry table, which does not do wonders for one's spine."

"I imagine it wouldn't," Utterson agreed amiably. "I shall tell Henry to expect you at three."

"Thank you."

Utterson left with a nod to myself and Erik, who, once Utterson's footsteps faded, broke his silence. "You are a masterful actor. I'd say your talents would be unparalleled on the stage."

I burst out laughing. "I've considered acting occasionally. Imagine what I could accomplish with time to prepare."

"I've no need to imagine. I saw what you were capable of in costume when you found Lucy. That alone would convince anyone of your talents." He stared at me, a serious expression easing over his features. "You are going to meet with Jekyll, then?"

"Yes. But I shall not give him the opportunity to

go on the offensive. This is one of the roads I hypothesized about last night. It shall be my only real chance to find out any details of what the HJ drugs do, directly from Jekyll. If I fail . . ." I sighed deeply. "If I fail . . . well, I'll cross that bridge when and if I come to it."

Worry flashed across Erik's eyes, but he said nothing. I couldn't help but wonder if his keen mind had discovered what I had planned if all else failed.

I found myself hoping that all else would not fail.

*****

I went alone to Jekyll's, arriving at about ten minutes to three. Poole showed me in and instructed me to go down the spiral staircase to the laboratory. Jekyll was expecting me there.

"Very well," I said with a curt nod. Though I was slightly apprehensive about going to the basement, at least that location guaranteed our privacy.

When I reached the bottom of the stairs, I saw the laboratory door was open, so I called out, "Jekyll? It is I, Sherlock Holmes."

"Yes. Come in, Holmes."

My eyebrows furrowed. I paused, my hand still on the railing. *Was* that Jekyll? The voice sounded deeper, raspier, like sandpaper on wood.

I hesitated long enough that Jekyll came to the doorway, once again looking haggard and run-down, with a slightly deeper tinge of insanity in his eyes. But of course, it was the same man. Perhaps I had imagined the change in his vocals. Or perhaps he'd simply worn out his voice one way or another.

"I do apologize for my hesitation. Stairs are not kind to a leg that is never at its best. Also, for a moment, you sounded like someone else."

He muttered something that sounded like, *"But for a moment, I almost was,"* but when I asked him to repeat himself, he refused. Instead, he looked at me and said, "Please, come in. I'm sure Utterson explained how eager I am to speak with you."

"Eager? Indeed. He indicated that you take me for nothing more than a common thief, suspecting me of breaking into this room. And to steal what, exactly? Utterson never specified."

"Do not act so innocent, Mr. Holmes! You are not so far above us that one cannot grasp you and expose you for the phony you are!"

"Indeed? And what, pray tell, am I being phony about?"

"I know you were looking around here when Lucy came, trying to figure out how to break in unseen. I don't know how you did it, but you came into this lab and stole something that I--"

"Yes? That you what?" I demanded.

"Nothing. It's something needed for an experiment, that's all. I require it back."

It was time to try my hand and learn what I could about the real connection between Jekyll and Hyde. "It seems to me, Jekyll," I replied coldly, "that the man you should search out and accuse is Hyde."

Jekyll glared at me with such animalistic ferocity I almost took a step back. But a feral instinct rose in my own gut and I met his eyes unflinchingly.

"*Never,*" he rasped, saliva pooling in the corners of his mouth, "accuse Hyde of such a thing. You know *nothing* of the man. Of what he's capable -- and not capable -- of doing."

"And do you so intimately know his limitations? He beat a young girl badly enough that she couldn't move for two days. He's murdered *your* fiancée's father and used a cane of yours to do the deed. A cane which you say you would not lend, and Hyde would not borrow. What is left but theft? Surely, then, it would not be such a stretch to imagine him breaking into your house and stealing another possession."

"No," he murmured, turning away from me and hunching over his chemistry table. "No, Hyde wouldn't dare. Not *that.* He--he wouldn't . . . dare . . ."

"Henry . . ." Remorse swept through me at pushing him so much. This man was being torn apart. I felt I was witnessing a breakdown before my eyes. "Please, I want to help you. And I am in a better position to do so than anyone else. I know you were ridiculed and denied by the Board at St. Jude, but I promise you, I will do no such thing. Please, tell me the details of your experiment. Your patient . . . Henry, surely you must realize that, perhaps from the start, but certainly now, your patient is no longer a patient, but a victim."

Jekyll gave me a resigned stare. "Yes, the patient is a victim. Of that, there is no doubt."

"And who is this victim?" Slowly, I approached him. "Henry, is it your father?"

"What?" Surprise flashed through his eyes and he let out a sarcastic laugh. "My father? My father died four days ago at seven in the evening."

"Dead? Then why are there no records of him, his stay, or his condition at St. Jude?"

"I have some sway with the hospital, despite the Board's insistence that I am a lunatic with immoral notions on the human condition. Immoral. And yet they let the ones they consider to be feeble-minded rot away in their 'institutions.' They are not institutions, but prisons! Prisons to put the ones who are prisoners to their minds away forever. They wanted my father forgotten, so I had his records destroyed right after their last rejection of my request. He no longer existed, except in my memory, anyway. Now, as far as the world is concerned, that is the *only* place he ever existed."

The sheer tragedy in his tone and of those statements profoundly struck me. I was close enough to him, I put my hand on his shoulder and said, "I am deeply sorry the world will never know of such a man."

"You sound almost sincere."

"I *am* sincere. Henry, I am not your adversary. I wish to help you. But no one can do that if you won't let us."

"Holmes . . . I do appreciate your offer. You've no idea how grateful I am for it, but . . . I cannot accept help. I have started this alone and I must finish it alone."

"Are you quite sure you're doomed to follow that kind of solitude? It is a dangerous line to walk, one you can easily slip off the path of."

"I know. Believe me, I know that better than you will ever believe."

"Who is your patient, Henry?"

He gave a tired-sounding laugh. "You wouldn't believe me even if I did tell you."

100

"Is it Hyde?" I pressed.

Another tired laugh, this one tinged with bitterness. "Hyde is neither patient nor victim, Holmes."

"Then what is he?"

Jekyll closed his eyes briefly, then winced, appearing to be in some amount of discomfort. "Not even I can adequately answer what Hyde is, Holmes." He winced again, letting out a low grunt as well. "Now," he said in a forced voice, "I must ask you to leave. Please. I find I am . . . suddenly feeling extremely unwell."

"Henry?" I tried to move a bit closer, but he doubled over and backed away from me.

"Please. Leave me! You can do nothing but harm right now!" he shouted, falling to his knees.

"Henry! Are you ill? Tell me what plagues you," I pleaded. I wanted to go to him, but instinct told me to stay away.

"No -- yes -- I'll be -- fine," he hissed through clenched teeth. "Please, just go. Go!" He wrenched himself up by clawing at the edge of his chemistry table and staggered to the farthest wall once he was unsteadily on his feet. Every fiber of my being wanted to stay and make sure he was all right, to stay and see exactly what it was that was happening to the man, but I did as he asked. Albeit slowly, but I did leave. As soon as I was outside the doorway of the laboratory, I heard Jekyll's skulking steps, and the door slammed shut and locked, completely closing me out.

When I got to the upstairs corridor that led to the spiral staircase, I saw Poole.

"Please, check on Jekyll," I said to him. "I'm sure he'll keep his door locked, but he was doubled over in pain when I left him. Though I wanted to, he would not permit me to stay."

Poole nodded. "Thank you for forewarning me. This has happened to him several times before, sir. Each time, though he looks like he is in agony, he insists he is fine. I must take him at his word, because each time, he has emerged several hours later looking pale, but healthy."

"Do you know if he is prone to ulcers, or any other stomach ailments?" I inquired. I knew such things wouldn't cause the reaction I saw, but perhaps Poole could give me a clue by unknowingly helping me eliminate what it wasn't.

"Not that I know of, sir, unless it's a recent development."

"Which is possible," I muttered. Aloud, I asked, "Were you aware that Jekyll senior has died?"

"Yes. I believe it was the evening of the twenty-fifth."

The twenty-fifth? Something stirred in the back of my mind, something about that date, but I lost it a moment later. I decided Poole could give me no conclusive help, so as I exited the house and hailed a cab, I found myself dreading what I would have to do back at Baker Street. A sense of fear filled me, the likes of which I'd never felt before and wished I would never have to feel again.

Erik greeted me from the couch when I walked in the door. "Was your time with Jekyll sufficient to make things clear?"

"Unfortunately, no. On the contrary, all it succeeded in doing was to make things murkier. Except for one thing."

"And what is that?"

I caned over to my chemistry set and held up Jekyll's vial. "I need you here with me when I do this."

Erik got to his feet. "Holmes . . ." he said warningly. "Do what?"

I looked down and saw an unused syringe. Picking it up, I held it and the vial in my right hand and used my left to roll up my right sleeve above my elbow.

"Holmes, what--?" Then he realized. "Holmes, what in Hell are you thinking? You can't inject that into your bloodstream!"

"It's the only way, Erik," I answered in a low voice, staring at the vial. The liquid inside was mesmerizing, in an odd sort of way. "It's the only way to find out what the serum does to a person. And I would not think to ask you or Watson to subject yourselves to this."

"No, there has to be another way. Holmes, please. Think about what you're doing. You don't know what--!"

"Precisely!" I finally shouted, cutting him off and glaring at him. "I *don't* know and I'm determined to find out! Erik . . ." My glare softened to a pleading expression. "I need to know."

Erik's face slowly went from angry horror to determined apprehension. He closed his eyes and carefully nodded his assent. When he opened them again, readiness had replaced any hint of fear. "Learn, Holmes. I'll be here."

I cleaned the inside of my elbow with an alcohol swab, filled the syringe with Jekyll's formula, and before I could second guess myself, plunged the needle into the crook of my arm, pressing the contents into my bloodstream.

.

Chapter Nine - The World Has Gone Insane

The moments leading up to Holmes stabbing the syringe into his arm -- no more than three heartbeat's time, I was sure -- seemed to last an eternity. I could hear nothing. I could taste and touch and smell nothing. The only sense left to me was sight and I was powerless to stop the mad motions I viewed.

How to describe this? He winced and bent over his arm as the needle punctured his skin. I saw his thumb push the end so that the formula was forced into his veins. I watched helplessly as he staggered to his knees and then collapsed on his right side on the floor. Finally, slowly, so very slowly, he got to his feet, bringing his cane with him.

"Holmes?" I said warily.

"I feel . . . nothing new. Well, my tongue feels a bit swollen. The injection point hurts. Hmm . . ." he puckered his lips several times. "An odd sensation in my . . ."

"Holmes?" A slight urgency entered my tone.

He looked at me. "Nothing. I'm fine, I assure you. Just a twinge. I'm really quite--" Suddenly, his eyes went wide enough that I could see white all the way around the iris. "Dear God," he gasped, as if all the oxygen was being forced from his lungs.

Before I was even able to say his name, Holmes dropped his cane and fell to his knees, then on his back, letting out a horrific shriek. I found, though now it was a different person making it, the sound was familiar; I'd heard it before as I knelt near the boarded up window to Jekyll's laboratory.

.

"Holmes!" I shouted worthlessly as I rushed to his side. He writhed on the floor like a man possessed. There was nothing I was capable of doing to be of any assistance! Not to mention the vague thought in the back of my mind that any minute, someone would open the door and believe a masked man was attempting to murder Sherlock Holmes.

He let out a second scream of pure agony and shudders ran down my spine even as his own stiffened. Then I was aware of footsteps coming up the stairs. My own eyes widened and I dashed madly for the door, locking it just in time.

"Mr. Holmes? Erik?" Mrs. Hudson called. "What's going on? Are you all right in there?"

"Yes, we're fine," I said, focusing on keeping my voice level and calm. "Holmes . . . stepped wrong and hurt his leg," I fabricated.

"Well, that scream was loud enough to wake the dead. Woke me out of a sound sleep, he did. I hope he's all right?"

So did I. I assured her he was, however, and she went back downstairs. All I could hear from Holmes was a heavy, rasping breathing.

"Holmes?" I said, turning around and resting my back against the door. I could not see him from where I stood.

"Is *that* my name?" he asked. I thought it was him, anyway. This did not sound like his regular voice. This voice was guttural, feral.

"Of course," I answered hesitantly. "Are . . . are you all right?"

"Fine, fine. I can assure you, I haven't felt this

alive in quite some time." Finally, he got to his feet.

I almost couldn't believe my eyes. Sherlock Holmes was a man who stood ramrod straight, shoulders back, chin up, and moved with grace and confidence even after his procurement of a cane. He would meet a man's eyes unflinchingly, and an undeniable spark of intelligence shone from his, as well as the sense of kindness and compassion he had for those he cared about.

The man in front of me, though . . . He almost appeared hunchbacked, with his shoulders curved forward, head bent down, giving anyone who looked the idea that he was a good six inches shorter than his true height. Even from how he stood, it was obvious he was favoring his right leg. This was no surprise, seeing as he wasn't using his cane. But his eyes . . . there was no warmth, no compassion, no *feeling* in them whatsoever. Just a vast, dark, wasteland of nothingness.

This was not the Sherlock Holmes Watson wrote about.

This was *not* the Sherlock Homes who challenged me in the opera house.

This was not *Sherlock Holmes.*

"Who are you?" I demanded, taking several strides toward him.

"You called me by my name yourself," he answered cruelly. "Now, you . . . Why do you wear a mask?"

He staggered toward me and I had to remind myself that somewhere inside this despicable creature was the Sherlock Holmes I had befriended and respected. Had I not, I'd surely have stepped away. I could not pinpoint why, but there was something about this man -- *this*

Holmes -- that instantly inspired hatred within me.

He pawed at my face with fingers twisted into claw-like hooks and I had to restrain myself from hitting him or violently pushing him away. Instead, I merely tried to cover my face with my arm, but he got to the mask first.

When he realized he was holding it, he inspected it coldly, then dropped it to the floor. I stood, muscles tense, my body ready to attack at the slightest provocation, my mind screaming at me to remain in control. He stared at my face, at the ruined right side, once coming so close that I could feel his moist, hot breath on my neck. When he finally stepped back, I relaxed, minutely, until he started to laugh.

It was a loud, cackling, sarcastic, cruel laugh, no different from any of the chortlings I heard when I was trapped in the Gypsy's carnival. I could feel the uncontrollable rage beginning to spread through me, so I ducked down to retrieve and replace my mask in order to have something to do with my hands other than wrapping them around his neck.

"You are a singularly ugly creature," he said. He staggered back towards the table, seeing the violin case and stooping to pick it up. "What is this?"

"Your violin," I said, my tone slipping into a cold one to match his. My nerves were crackling with anticipation. I knew how much that violin meant to Holmes. To the *real* Holmes.

"Interesting," he rasped, removing it from its case. He fingered the strings for a moment before grabbing the neck and the bottom of the instrument and, amazingly quickly, bring it up and then down on to his right -- *raised* -- knee.

"No!" I cried at the moment of impact. Too late, I found myself able to move. I grabbed the violin from him, with no resistance because he was already letting it slip to the floor, and inspected the damage. Damn this man who hunched in front of me, there was no way to repair it!

He stumbled toward the door, more dragging his right leg than stepping with it. When I saw him put his hand on the doorknob, I was spurred to action again.

"What are you doing?" I demanded, moving so I could block him from exiting.

He let out another guttural chuckle that made my blood run cold. Instead of answering, he made as if to duck down. When I made the mistake of leaning a bit closer to him, he swung his left hand out and caught me on my upper cheek and temple. I stumbled back, falling, and hit my other temple on the corner of Holmes's chair.

The last thing I saw before slipping into unconsciousness was him, framed by the open doorway, about to escape into the night.

*****

"Erik! Erik, wake up!" was the first thing I heard, coming back to consciousness.

"Huh? What?" I said. My speech sounded garbled and far away to my ears. I slowly looked to where the other voice had come from and saw Watson. "Watson! I have to--" I tried to sit up, but a wave of dizziness swept over me and I slumped forward into Watson's waiting hands.

"You must sit still," he said, every inch the doctor now. He stared intently at my pupils. "You undoubtedly suffered a concussion and I don't know how long you were unconscious. Talk to me, tell me what happened here. How much do you remember?"

I looked to my right and saw the used syringe on the floor under Holmes's chemistry table. Closer to me was his violin, now in two splintered pieces. "Oh, God . . . and he's escaped. He's out there somewhere. We have to find him!" I struggled to sit up, but Watson somehow held me in one place.

"Who escaped? Erik, please, what is--?" He stopped and his face paled. "Erik, did Hyde come here?"

"Hyde? No, Hyde--" I took in a sharp breath as an epiphany hit me. *"Hyde."*

Watson took my realization to mean I was addled and spoke to me as though I was a young child. "Yes, Erik. A man named Hyde that Holmes told us about recently."

It took every inch of my willpower not to yell at Watson. He didn't know what had happened, I reminded myself.

"Yes, I remember who Hyde is. I think I've realized something, not needed my memory refreshed."

"I apologize. What did you realize?"

I opened my mouth to answer, but it dawned on me that my burst of anger at him had completely knocked the thought from my head. It had to do with Hyde. And something about how Holmes was right now . . . My eyes widened. Holmes!

"Holmes," I said instead. "Holmes is . . . not himself right now." I quickly explained how he'd injected himself with Jekyll's serum, and the resulting actions. "When you mentioned Hyde, well, Holmes's description of the man fits what Holmes has become."

"What Holmes has become? Erik, you speak as if Holmes is two people. Are you sure you're not more injured than I thought? You could have a more serious malady than I initially presumed. Perhaps you're hallucinating."

"I admit I've hit my head. I have the bumps to prove it. But I know of what I speak." I looked at him and then motioned to the violin pieces. "You know how highly I value music and you know how much Holmes prizes his violin. But look! What other explanation could there be but the serum causing an alter ego of Holmes to emerge?"

Watson gazed forlornly at the shattered pieces of Holmes's instrument. "There are many," he said finally. "Holmes has often said that one must eliminate all possibilities and whatever is left, however improbable, is the solution. We have not yet begun to eliminate all the possibilities. But, as Holmes would, I will trust your word."

Sighing with relief, I said, "Thank you, Watson. Now, whichever solution is the truth, the fact remains that Holmes must be found."

"What are we to do, then? How will we catch up to him?"

"We split up, patrol the streets. I more than know how to sink into the mind of a madman. But if you find him, do not approach him. Bring a revolver with you and shoot up in the air. I'll be able to find you."

"Don't approach him? Erik, surely Holmes isn't that dangerous?"

More slowly this time, I sat up. Then I took the

front of Watson's shirt in my fist and brought his face inches from mine so we were eye to eye. "Holmes hit me hard enough -- with his *left* hand, I might add -- that I was knocked off-balance enough to fall. Could the Holmes you're familiar with be capable of such violence?"

"Why the emphasis on --" he stopped, catching my implication, and said in a dead voice, "Holmes is not left-handed."

"Precisely." Gingerly, I touched the bumps on the sides of my head. Painful, but I could manage. "Now, if you could help me to my feet, we must go after him."

"His cane," Watson said, noticing it on the floor by the chemistry table. "But . . . how does he walk?"

"He more drags his leg than steps with it. Leave the cane, but bring a revolver."

Still skeptical, but trusting my words regardless, he assisted me in standing, then got a revolver from a hidden compartment in Holmes's desk.

"Remember what I said. If you find him, stay hidden, and shoot up into the sky. I'll find you."

"And if you find him first?"

I had no revolver. I had no need of one. Not when I had the Punjab lasso with me, which I was reaching for to tuck into the pocket of the cloak I wrapped around my shoulders. Silence was my best answer, because not even I knew what my actions would be upon contact with that man again.

"It is almost midnight now," he said a moment later. "If I have nothing to show for my efforts in an hour's time, I'll come back here and wait. You have a much better chance of finding someone in this oppressive darkness, anyhow."

I nodded. "That's a suitable plan."

Starting for the door, I paused briefly when I heard Watson say, "Be careful, Erik."

"You, too, Watson, " I answered before slipping out into the night.

*****

I don't know why I was drawn first to the Red Rat. Perhaps it was because that was where I first saw Jekyll. Perhaps it was because that's where Holmes went first to find out what he could about Lucy, and therefore it was the starting point of the mystery for him in two ways. Or perhaps it was that I let the madman within me take over and was operating on nothing more than instinct.

Soon enough, from the alleyway where I first saw Jekyll and Lucy meet, I spotted him. His gait was unmistakable, dragging his right leg behind him, staggering along at an uneven, limping pace. I was reaching for my lasso to subdue him when I saw the other figure approach. At first, I was worried Watson had paid no heed to my warnings after all, but then the second man walked by one of the gaslights. I only caught a glimpse, but it was enough to bring a surge of hatred to the forefront of my mind. I'd only felt that immediate sense of hate once before, several hours ago when Holmes approached me to claw at my mask. This second man had to be Hyde.

They stopped in front of one another and each eyed the other warily. I had the vague impression of wolves circling, about to do battle to determine which was the dominant male. Tightening my grip on the lasso, I waited, muscles taut.

"And who are you?" Hyde finally rasped. They both had that same husky, primitive tone to their voices.

"I was told my name is Holmes," he answered. "Why should one of your --" he smirked, disdainfully, "station care?"

"Do not test the limits of my temper. I have killed once; I doubt you would relish being my second victim."

"You are that confident you could overpower me? Go ahead. You're welcome to try." I could hear the mocking invitation in his voice.

Hyde looked tempted and I prepared to jump out of the shadows and in between them. But he stepped back and glared at the other man. I found I could not think of him as Holmes.

"We shall meet again, Holmes. Then we will see who comes out the victor."

The other started to laugh as Hyde walked away. As I watched his disappearance into the shadows, I saw what the maid must have observed. There truly was a certain unidentifiable aspect of deformity about the man. As soon as Hyde was out of sight, that maniacal laugh turned to a choking cough and the other fell to his knees. Stupidly dropping my lasso, I ran to his side.

When he saw me, his eyes gleamed with recognition. "Erik! Erik, I--!" Another stream of coughs wracked his frame, and I carefully took hold of him and eased him onto his back to give relief to his leg.

Minutes later, after the coughing fits and muscle spasms subsided, an exhausted Holmes looked up at me.

"That was a Hellish ordeal," he said weakly.

I tightened my arms around his shoulders

comfortingly, easing him up to a sitting position. "You're very good at understatement, my friend."

Holmes glanced around. "I'm no longer at Baker Street."

"No."

"My cane is not here."

"No."

"When did I leave 221B?"

"I'm . . . unsure. It must have been several hours ago at this point," I said.

"Why are you unsure?"

"Because I . . . was unconscious for an unknown period tonight."

"Unconscious? Erik, who--?" He stopped, slumping back against my arm. "I did it."

"Yes."

"Erik, please accept my apology. I was not myself."

"I know, Holmes. I know. There's no need to explain. We do need to get you home, however. If I give assistance, do you think you can walk?"

"I'll attempt."

I pulled Holmes to his feet, positioning myself on his right side and supporting him so as little weight as possible was shifted to his right leg as he walked. It was very tedious and slow-going, and we had to stop numerous times so Holmes could rest and I could stretch my back and shoulders, but finally we made it back to Baker Street around two in the morning.

Once inside, Holmes collapsed on the couch and gripped his thigh, which I knew must be causing him agony. Watson was soundly asleep in the chair, revolver positioned in his hand, pointed at the floor. Carefully, I removed it and put it on the desk. Then, I got some more of my herbs and quickly mixed them into a cup of tea for Holmes to give him a respite from the pain.

Three quarters of an hour later, the tea was gone and both men were soundly asleep. I stayed awake, holding the broken pieces of Holmes's prized violin, staring out the window until the dawn began to break through the blackness.

Chapter Ten - Good and Evil

For several days, I didn't know precisely what had happened to me. Erik had described what he saw, and in great detail, but I could not strike an equilibrium between who I knew I was, and the monster Erik was depicting.

Or, who I *thought* I was.

Watson was wrong to confirm Erik's thoughts that I am not left-handed. I am actually what is called ambidextrous. I am an ambidextrous person who favors his right hand for everyday tasks, though. Apparently, when under the influence of the serum, the hand I favor changed. Erik informed me that I lashed out at him with my left hand. Something that, if I had done it as I am now, would have been more than coordinated enough to connect (after all, to keep up my physical dexterity, I had not only mastered fencing, but also boxing), but would not normally have had the power behind it to knock Erik off his feet from so awkward an angle.

I recall waking up the next morning to find that my leg was stiff, but in no more pain than usual. As I rubbed the sleep from my eyes, I automatically reached for my cane. My fingers failed to find it. When I fully opened my eyes and gazed around, I saw it on the floor by my chemistry table and Erik standing by the window, staring out and holding . . .

"Erik, what do you have?" I asked softly. Watson was still snoring in the chair.

Erik turned and regarded me sadly. "Your violin. I'm so sorry, Holmes."

For a moment, I mistook his apology and thought

he was admitting his own guilt. But a flash of memory enveloped me as I opened my mouth. Me, holding the violin, then bringing it down on my upraised knee.

Look for the evidence, my mind whispered. I reached down and pulled up my right trouser leg to examine my knee. There was a slight bruise just above the kneecap and when I straightened my trouser leg, I found small slivers of polished wood stuck in the material.

Erik wasn't admitting his guilt; he was apologizing for my loss.

"Oh, God . . . how could I . . . ?"

Erik stepped over to the couch, depositing the splintered remains in my hands when I reached for them. "You were not yourself, Holmes. It was as if a different person inhabited your body."

"Whether or not that is true, it was still these hands that destroyed such a beautiful instrument."

"Indeed. I cannot deny that. But it was not your mind."

I considered his words. "Yes. From what I do recall, I had the distinct sensation that I was in the background of my own actions and decisions. It's almost . . . I suppose I could say this part of me -- the rational, thinking part -- had gone dormant. And if that occurs, what is there left but instinct, cruelty, and the base needs of a human?"

Erik nodded. "The distinction isn't usually so stark, however, as it was with you."

That statement hung between us until our eyes met.

"Cruelty . . ." I murmured.

"Instinct . . ." he echoed my tone.

"Base needs . . . let's say from a prostitute."

"Hyde!" we shouted in unison.

"Wha--? Hide what?" Watson, still half-asleep and woken mid-snore, said.

I smiled. "Sorry, old chap. We didn't mean to wake you."

"I doubt we did. He's already back to sleep," Erik observed.

"He should rest. I'm sure I provided you both with nothing but anger, panic, and worry last night." Not to be completely derailed from my train of thought, I said, "Hyde, though."

"Yes. This was the epiphany that shimmered in my mind last night. Watson distracted me and I had just woken from my rather unpleasant concussion, so the thought didn't stick. Jekyll's experiment means that Hyde has an alter ego. But how do we find out who it is?"

"We don't need to find out," I said slowly. "We already know who it is. He's been in front of us the entire time."

"What? I'm afraid I don't follow you."

"Erik, don't you see? Jekyll's secretiveness, his non-sanctioned patient, the screams, Erik! The screams that were Jekyll's voice, but distorted. And suddenly his sentiment to me makes so much more sense. He told me he had started this alone, and that he must finish it alone."

"Dear God . . ." Erik breathed. "You're saying that Jekyll . . ."

" . . . *is* Hyde."

*****

118

Here are some of the pages from Jekyll's journal, included to make the timeline more complete, and to explain a few things. Some notes of mine are included.

August 23rd, 3:00 pm

I've procured the last of the chemicals which I believe will give me a base potent enough for use in humans. My rudimentary testing is concluded. HJ-R-14 was successful in the rodents. Results recorded.

*My next step is to send an exact copy of my findings as well as an outline explaining what it all means to the Board of Directors. They cannot ignore me once they see this. They cannot ignore the good it will do mankind. They will **have** to grant me a human subject.*

What results could he have reached with rodents? And perhaps the success came because their brains are so simplistic, especially compared to human beings who plan and feel and use logic.

How would he know he truly had success?

It is unfortunate he doesn't record his results in this journal.

September 12th, 5:00 pm

Damn those bastards on the Board! They are all hypocritical cowards, every miserable one of them!

I forget myself. Sir Danvers is not. Yet even he wishes me to concede my experiments. Why do they not see that were this to work on a patient in an asylum, it could revolutionise how we view mental illness? All I ask for is a forgotten soul that society has given up on! All I ask . . . all I ask for is the ability to save my father, if no one else. He is in there, I know, ultimately kidnapped and tortured by the disease that ravages his once brilliant mind.

I must continue these musings and rants later, if I'm to be ready for Emma's and my engagement party at the Carew's tonight.

September 13th, 11:50 pm

I have just come from a place called the Red Rat, where prostitutes and other unfortunates of the London streets linger, and I met an exceptional woman named Lucy. We spoke. She propositioned me, but I refused. I have Emma to think of. However, I sensed something more in this young Unfortunate. There is most definitely something special about her. I wonder what life dealt her that she found herself in such a compromising position. I did give her my card, promising if she ever needed a friend - and only that - to come to me.

I find I am drawn to Lucy. Despite her situation in life, she retains a spark. Not something often associated with 'ladies of the night.'

She makes me wonder . . .

-11:56 pm

I have reached my decision. Seven years ago, I began this endeavor alone and that is how I must complete it. The Board has refused me a patient numerous times. They refuse to sanction a candidate, even though I ask for one of London's forgotten, one who has been placed in their institution with no hope of recovery. No hope from any of them, anyway. I, however, retain an immense sense of hope. And to that end, I must use myself as the subject of the experiment.

-11:58 pm

Injected vial of HJ-1 into my veins. Entered through the left arm, at the inside of the elbow. No real changes in sensation yet. A strange, sweet warmth seems to spread through my veins. My tongue feels swollen. Slight fuzzy feeling in my brain. No noticeable behavioral differences.

-MIDNIGHT

FREE!

This must be Hyde's handwriting,
for it slopes slightly to the left and
is much messier. Perhaps Jekyll is
right-handed and Hyde is left-handed?

September 27th, 2pm

Damn this experiment! Two days ago, I radically altered the formula in an attempt to control Hyde's evil influence, but it has backfired on me! I learned of my father's death and it caused me such anguish that at half-past eight, I transformed again!

In thinking upon things from a somewhat rational standpoint, as I have vowed to do concerning these transformations, I believe the reason for this one came about on its own (without the serum,) because I was in such a state of grief.

God in Heaven, how can I attempt logic and rationality after what I've done?! As Hyde, I went to find Lucy. She seemed to vaguely recognize Hyde, yet he assured her they'd never met. He bought her for the night but, after he injured her to the point of immobility, he left in disgust. He prowled the streets for about two hours, and then saw Sir Danvers Carew on the street. I believe his rage stemmed from my own grief of just having lost my father. Why should Emma have one when I am alone in the world? I began this Hellish experiment to **save** my father, but he was taken by the cold hand of Death instead.

Hyde attacked Sir Danvers with a fervor and a sense of detachment I have never known before. Then, he came back to my laboratory, injected himself so I could take control again, and left me to remember the horrible things this beast inside me has done. I was so distraught, I stayed up the entire night, creating more HJ combinations. I finally came up with HJ-7 and HJ-8, the latest formulas that may eradicate Hyde forever. I only wish I could be sure that would be the final result. There are things extremely worrisome about the transformations, especially this one. I did not need the serum to become Hyde. The experiment is only in its third week! How could the serum have absorbed so fully into my body? Of course, I have increased the potency, but for the sake of control over the evil side of my mind. Hyde . . . his influence is growing, not only in my sleeping mind, but in my waking. I must admit, I have an immense fear that the formulas are not as potent as they could be, because Hyde does not want to be destroyed. He wants to gain control, and to that end, what will the next injection do? I'm terribly afraid to find out, but I more fear stopping the experiment at this stage. If I did, what more would Hyde do? Bringing us back into unity is out of the question. Hyde has performed too heinous an act. He **must** be destroyed before he can consume me.

He emerges from the darkest depths of my soul to wreak havoc on the innocent, then escapes back inside me, no more substantial than a stain of breath upon a mirror.

He has the perfect hiding place . . .

I did not need more than one injection to transform independently of the formula.

Perhaps this says something about how strong Jekyll was making the serum. Or perhaps it depends from person to person and hinges upon the strength of the mind, or possibly the expectation of the formula. Jekyll knew his intent, and therefore had a possibly easier time keeping control.

-4 PM

INDEED. INSIDE THIS PATHETIC FOOL'S BODY RESTS THE PERFECT HIDING PLACE. AND I WILL NOT BE SO EASILY MANIPULATED. I KNOW THAT APPALLING EXCUSE FOR A MAN WANTS TO RID HIMSELF OF ME.

I WON'T BE GOTTEN RID OF SO EASILY. AND IF IT TAKES MORE MURDERS TO SHOW THAT TO JEKYLL, THEN I WILL HAPPILY KILL AGAIN.

-7:34 pm

Sherlock Holmes is wrong. How dare he

insinuate Hyde steal my formula? That formula is the very reason for his existence! He would do nothing to compromise that situation!

Besides, every time I've transformed, I've still retained some sense of consciousness. In the very recesses of my mind, perhaps, but I've always been present, been aware of what was happening, even if I could not control the actions myself.

But then . . . I just noticed the page before this stuck to the one prior. Now I see why. There was ink on it, dried into place because someone – Hyde – had written an entry and pressed the page down to purposely catch. From the time, I'd say he wrote it shortly after Mr. Holmes left my laboratory.

Dear God. I . . . I don't remember him writing this.

I don't remember . . .

-11:42 PM

AH, SO MY 'BETTER' SELF IS WORRIED, IS HE? THINKS THAT I MAY ALTER THE FORMULA SOMEHOW? HE *SHOULD* BE! I KNOW HIS THOUGHTS, AND EDWARD HYDE IS NOT ONE SO EASILY DESTROYED!

*****

Over the next week, I did extensive testing on the few drops left in Jekyll's vial, as well as the small portion I'd already extracted to inspect. I learned that Watson had seen nothing of my transformation and I was not eager to describe the sensation to him. Erik, as well, remained strangely silent, merely keeping up an almost twenty-four hour straight vigil to watch over me each day. I encouraged him to sleep, but when he insisted he was fine, I said nothing else to deter him from his course. I was glad he was doing it, for I didn't feel quite myself during that period. There were times of complete normalcy, but then there were others . . .

How to describe the sensation? It felt like someone was scurrying around in my head, but never quite slowly enough for me to pinpoint his location. Sometimes, especially when tired or stressed, I felt a push in my head, like he was trying to get out. It was times like that when I could have most used Erik's beautiful violin playing. Alas, my alter did not appear to care for music and I had been unable thus far to procure a suitable replacement. Luckily, the realization that I had no violin didn't provide me with more stress. It actually helped me be angry at the monster inside my head, thus making control easier.

On October third, I had an interesting conversation with Erik, concerning madness. I'd had a particularly frustrating day at my chemistry set, unable to decipher anything new about the makeup of chemicals Jekyll had used, so finally I collapsed in my chair, lit my pipe, and asked him, "What do you make of insanity?"

"Hmm?" he murmured, looking at me through quizzical and sleepy eyes.

"Madness. Insanity. What sense do you make of it?" I asked, feeling bad that I was evidently keeping him from much needed sleep.

Erik sighed, rubbed his eyes, and stretched his arms above his head, arching his back. When he was finished, he said, "Only that there truly is no sense to it."

"There must be," I argued. "A degree, a measure, something by which one can compare."

"Compare what?" he challenged. "By what measure would you put my actions at the opera house? Or yours several nights ago? Or Jekyll's for creating -- or perhaps just releasing -- Hyde? When all this began, you said sanity was relative and used yourself and your odd habits as an example. You're only realizing now *how* relative and tenuous sanity truly is. You didn't know the price some have to pay."

"I do now," I said.

Sighing again, Erik replied, "No. I'm afraid you don't. You are grappling with madness, I will not contest that. But you won't fully realize the price you've paid until the battle is over."

"Until I come back from it, or it consumes me, you mean."

"Yes."

Turning that over in my mind, I was quiet for several minutes before asking, "How did you come back?"

He looked down at his hands, clasped knuckles facing up in front of him. Just when I was sure he wasn't going to answer, he said, "How do you know I did come back?"

"Erik . . ."

"I'm serious, Holmes. How do you know I'm not still the obsessed madman that I was down in the lair beneath the opera house? Simply because I'm in a different setting? Or perhaps because I haven't mentioned Christine?"

"No. It's because *you* are different. Your mannerisms, your speech, your thoughts, they are all changed since the opera house."

"Ah, but I could just be a very good actor. You and Jekyll, you've both had a chemical separation occur in your brains. For others, the distinction is not so sharp. Good and evil are never so black and white."

"All right, yes, I see your point."

But Erik was relentless. He moved over so he was standing before me. "Do you? As I said in my letter, you never know what is lurking beneath the surface. The ones who give off the sanest appearance can be hiding the cruelest madman underneath. How can you truly judge if one has come back from that brink? Sometimes the 'madmen' themselves cannot even judge that correctly.

And certainly not without a bias."

"Erik. Please, stop! I understand."

He took his seat again. "Do you, Holmes? For all your intelligence, can you truly grasp the answer?" He looked me straight in the eye and said, "You extended your hand to me. You asked me to become your partner. Did I accept?"

"No. You physically threw me from your lair."

"Precisely. You could not save me. You couldn't bring me back from the brink. I had to make that decision. I had to face myself and decide to continue fighting."

"And have you?" I asked, uncertain now that he had indicated otherwise.

He smiled behind the mask. "Yes, Holmes. That is why I came to you. I looked at myself, at my situation, at what I had become and what I could still become if I didn't fight. I did not, *would* not, let complete insanity take over."

"I'm glad."

Erik went to the window and looked out. "You see, that's what most people don't realize. And never realize. Murder, carnage, madness? Those things are easy. A madman can commit murder because he's truly beyond the point of caring if he's caught. He's given up and is going by what instinct tells him to do. The most difficult thing for a man to do in this life is to live it, and live it well. We all have circumstances that are -- at best -- unfavorable to us." Here, his fingers lightly touched the mask that hid his face. "We can blame others for the misfortune that befalls us, or we can take charge of our own destiny and continue that never-ending uphill battle."

"The battle of intelligence over base instinct."

He turned and stared at me. "The battle of holding on to sanity even when one wants to let it go."

The general meaning of our conversation and Erik's soliloquy was crystal clear: I had a battle ahead, and it was one that, while Erik would be close by, I would have to fight alone.

Considering that I knew I had a lunatic prowling around in my head, I looked to this battle with nothing but trepidation and apprehension.

Chapter Eleven - Streak of Madness

And I was right to do so. On October seventh, Watson, Erik, and I were seated in various places around 221B around eight in the evening, discussing different hypotheses concerning Jekyll and Hyde. Watson was completely filled in, though he was still skeptical that a person's mind could be so thoroughly split through chemical means. Erik kept assuring him that it was true, it was exactly what had happened to me, but when Watson would turn to me for confirmation, I found I could give no definitive answer. I could not bring myself to tell him that I had indeed become such a ruthless madman. That the Sherlock Holmes he was so familiar with had utterly vanished for that brief period of time, and in my usual place was someone so animalistic, so barbaric that it sickened me. It was distressing to know Erik had seen me this way. Though I was thankful to him, I found it gave me a sense of debt. That I somehow owed him something, for seeing me in that condition and not having me committed. However, when I rationally considered things, I knew he would never let that thought cross his mind. After all, no doctor could help me. They, save Jekyll, who was probably worse off than I because he was traveling this path alone, would no doubt react just as Watson had. With disbelief, or worse. The only reason Watson took the news as well as he did was because it was me. Someone else, he would have insisted they be examined and observed, if not totally locked away.

To all our surprise, we were interrupted by Mrs. Hudson, who had a frantic-looking Emma Carew behind her.

"Mr. Holmes," Mrs. Hudson said, "Miss Carew insists upon seeing you, she--"

"Mr. Holmes, please! It's urgent!"

Mrs. Hudson must have already tried to tell her I would see no one. Yet how could I refuse the woman when she looked so panicked? Especially when her fiancé was doing the same thing to her? I glanced at Erik and Watson, then back to the doorway. "It's all right, Mrs. Hudson. Miss Carew, you may enter."

"Thank you." She scooted past the housekeeper and into the room, where Watson stood and offered her his chair. She sank into it gratefully.

Erik cleared his throat. "What can we do for you, Miss Carew? This is a rather inappropriate time for a social call--"

"I quite agree," she interrupted. "But it's not a social call. I've paid a visit to Henry. Yesterday, very late, around half-past eleven at night. Poole let me in. The laboratory door was unlocked, and I--I--"

She seemed on the verge of panicking, making me feel edgy. I closed my eyes and took a few deep breaths, feeling Erik's eyes on me. I also heard Watson ask Miss Carew if she would like something to help calm her down.

"No. No, I'm sorry. This has just upset me a great deal."

"Would you rather come back another time?" Erik asked.

"I'm worried what would happen if I don't say this now," she responded.

Opening my eyes again, I focused on Miss Carew. "All right. So you need to tell us now. Please, try your

134

best to relate the facts and not ramble into hysteria. You're here, I'm willing to listen, but not through bursts of random emotion."

Watson looked at me, shocked. While I'm quite sure what I said was rude, it also accomplished my goal. Miss Carew sat up straighter and composed herself brilliantly.

"I do apologize. The facts are these: around half-past eleven last evening, I went to Henry's residence. Poole let me in, though neither of us saw any sign of Henry. I assured Poole I was fine on my own and he went about his business. I quickly grew bored and went down the stairs to Henry's laboratory door. To my surprise, it was unlocked, so I entered. On his chemistry table was his journal, open to a new page. On the previous one, he'd written 'October sixth, ten forty-five pm. Here we stand, alone, trapped in this nightmare. More terrible than beasts that stalk prey for sustenance.'

"I read it aloud to myself because I couldn't at first comprehend that he would write something so disturbing. I suppose I felt my eyes were playing tricks on me and hearing the words spoken aloud was the only way to prove to myself that I actually saw those two terrible lines. That was when Henry found me. There is a back entrance to his laboratory, where you can enter directly from the road. He came in and accused me of spying on him. I told him that all I wished for was some word from him. That I've been exceedingly worried these past few weeks. He remained silent, but fine tremors traveled up and down his arms, and he held his back in a very rigid way, as if trying to control something. What, I can't imagine."

I shared a look with Erik. We could imagine

exactly what Jekyll was trying to keep under control.

"He told me his work was taking some very unexpected turns, and that his compulsion to continue was like an addiction. He said the truth was in there, but he seemed to be trying to convince himself of it as much as me. I knelt down beside him to try and assure him that I never expected the path he wanted was going to be easy or pleasant, but that we could take this journey together. He gripped my hand for a moment, but then pulled away, going to the other side of the laboratory. He breathed very heavily for a few moments, then said to me, 'Emma, please don't abandon me. I need you now, more than you know. And you may have faith in this: I *do* love you.'"

She stopped speaking. Erik cleared his throat and asked, "What did you answer?"

"I said . . . I said that if he needed me, or perhaps when he needed me, he knew where I'd be. Then, I left his laboratory. I admit, I'm not sure what you can do with this information, but I felt I needed to tell someone. I could not deal with this all on my own."

"Yes, you were right to come to us, Miss Carew," I said. "We were discussing different hypotheses where Jekyll is concerned, but they are of a somewhat delicate, private nature. Perhaps Mrs. Hudson could offer you some tea downstairs?"

She stared at the three of us for a moment, perhaps attempting to size up whether she wanted to demand to hear our thoughts. But then she nodded. "Yes. Tea would be lovely. I'll see myself out. Goodnight, gentlemen. Thank you for listening."

We bid her farewell and as soon as the door was closed, Erik said, "This is an interesting development."

"Indeed," I agreed. "Jekyll can't bear to tell anyone what's going on, but he does not want Miss Carew to forsake him."

"But even with what she told us, what can we do?" Watson asked.

"We cannot properly help Jekyll until my own mind is back in one piece," I said, coming full circle in our conversation. "He's determined to continue his experiment alone, but considering the vials I saw in his laboratory, he's not having the success he wants."

"What if we were to explain what has happened to you?" Watson asked. "Perhaps he would be willing to work with us?"

"Would he believe us? Especially since I led him to believe Hyde had . . ."

"Holmes? Why did you stop?" Watson asked.

"I . . . led Jekyll to believe that Hyde was the logical choice to have sneaked in and stolen the HJ formula. He nearly panicked, and now I understand why. Hyde must have been nearing the point where he was acting completely independently of Jekyll."

"Dear God, Holmes!" Watson cried. "I know that you follow unorthodox methods to achieve the end of a case, but this--"

"I'm aware, Watson," I said sharply. "I did it not with malicious intent, but in the hopes of forcing Jekyll to reveal information. And had I known beforehand that Jekyll and Hyde were one, I would never have suggested it."

"It cannot be taken back now," Erik said. "But it does raise an interesting question. What if that exchange has made Jekyll worse?"

My eyes widened. "Perhaps we should speak with him. Unfortunately, we don't know how volatile of a state he is in right now. We don't know what would set Hyde off to emerge. He is not someone I wish to encounter at the present time. I cannot risk my own alter ego emerging."

Erik nodded his agreement and Watson could not come up with a suitable argument to sway either of us.

"We are on our own," I said. "How I wish I knew the finer points of what Jekyll is trying to accomplish! If we just had that clue, it would make things all the easier. With that knowledge, I may be able to figure out the combination of these rare chemicals that is needed. As it is, I am doing nothing but guesswork!"

Mrs. Hudson interrupted before either of them could give a reply. "Mr. Holmes?" she said, gently knocking on the door.

"Yes, Mrs. Hudson?"

She opened the door slightly, barely poking her head in. "Sorry to bother you again, sir, but Miss Carew left moments ago and when I showed her to the door, someone was standing there about to knock. They left me this package for you."

"Come in, please," I said, caning to the door. "You are not bothering us, I assure you. Who gave this to you?"

"He didn't give his name, sir, but he was mighty strange. He ordered me to deliver this package to you immediately."

"Strange? What made him strange?"

"I couldn't rightly say. He had an unsavory look about him and stood kind of hunched over. I don't know why, I'm not a woman prone to judging others, you see, but I took an instant dislike to him."

Erik's and my eyes met. "Hyde," we said in unison.

She handed me the parcel and left the room. I believe she still wondered about the story Erik concocted about me falling and injuring my leg. And I know that when the gunshot wound initially occurred, I became rather beastly to everyone in the vicinity. She was probably afraid I would become that kind of monster again. I almost gave a humorless laugh at the notion. If she only knew . . . I'd actually become something much more terrible.

I caned back to where I'd been sitting, holding the parcel. "I suppose he came to us first. I can't imagine what Hyde would leave me, however."

"From what you've described, I'm not sure I'd want to imagine," Watson said. I got the impression he was remembering seeing Carew's body.

"Indeed," I agreed. I undid the string and unfolded the thick brown paper from around the contents, instantly regretting doing so.

"Is that a lock of hair?" Watson said.

"There's a note underneath," Erik observed.

Carefully withdrawing the paper, I set aside the rest of the package on a nearby end table. I unfolded the somewhat slick, stained paper and several long, thread-like pieces fell into my lap.

"Those are pieces of the rope from my lasso," Erik noted.

"This does not bode well . . ." I leaned forward and picked up the lock of brown hair that appeared to be tied with a slick, red ribbon. When I touched it, though, it did not feel like material, and my fingers came away red.

I put my index and middle fingers to my nose and inhaled gently. It was faint, but there was the unmistakable coppery scent that was always associated with blood.

"Holmes?" Watson spoke hesitantly.

"Who was his victim this time?" Erik asked, already having assimilated the pieces.

"Victim?" Watson asked.

"Yes. He has killed again. I estimate this binding around the lock of hair to be a piece of the small intestine."

Watson looked more closely. "My God, you're right! That fiend!"

"What does the note say?" Erik asked.

I looked at the note, also stained with blood, and saw:

HE TRIED TO WARN HER AS WELL. BUT I AM THE STRONGER NOW. I SAID WE WOULD MEET AGAIN. LET US NOW SEE WHO THE VICTOR IS. I WILL BE WAITING AT THE RED RAT.

I threw the note aside. "He has murdered Lucy and is trying to use that fact to get me to meet with him so he may challenge me, undoubtedly in a fight to the death."

"He knows I was there that night, as well."

I looked at Erik. "Why do you say that?"

"Why else include threads from my lasso? I

dropped it the night you first transformed. Hyde must have gone back and picked it up."

"Which means he also followed us," I realized. "There would be no other way for him to know where to leave this package."

"Yes, there would be," Erik contradicted. "You told Hyde your name. It would be easy enough, with your reputation, to find out where you reside, whether he was seen as Jekyll or as Hyde."

"Damn," I said. I began to feel an odd sensation behind my eyes. Almost a pulsing sensation, like something pushing.

Pushing? I quickly realized what that meant. My alter ego was trying to emerge. But this time, instead of resisting, I felt myself wanting to give in. Wanting to set that other part of myself free. After all, how was I truly any better than Hyde? I'd spoken with Lucy, once in disguise and once at Jekyll's; she'd told us both about being attacked, and then gave the name Edward Hyde to Jekyll right in front of me. Yet did I warn her? Did I try to sympathize with her plight? Even Jekyll, distracted as he was, tried to truly connect with her. I was so obsessed with learning Hyde's name that it never crossed my mind to make sure she knew how serious the situation was and to warn her properly!

Erik's and Watson's voices faded into the background as a battle raged in my mind. If I had to make sense of it, which I was barely able to do later, I would describe it as two separate voices clashing, the conversation going something like this:

Him: Good riddance. One less dirty whore for the world to be contaminated by.

Me: She was a person! A young lady misfortune had fallen on. She did *not* deserve this kind of end.

Him: So I suppose you believe you could have prevented it?

Me: I *should* have prevented it! I knew who and what Hyde was days ago. I should have done something more. Found her, warned her, told her to leave the city.

Him: But you didn't. You stayed here, uselessly fooling with your chemicals in a futile attempt to keep me at bay.

Me: What do you mean futile? I haven't transformed since--"

Him: But you will! I *will* escape somehow. It's only a matter of time. I'm part of your consciousness, too. You decided to separate us and you don't know which traits have remained in you and which have transferred to me. Perhaps I'm the action taker in you. Which is why you did nothing and let that whore *die!*

Me: No! I would *not* have merely stood by while someone was murdered.

Him: Then what did you do to help her? Really help her, so that she could have lived?

I wracked my brain. There had to be something, some way that I had, in fact, assisted her, but my memory was coming up blank. All it would hand me were evidences that there had been something else I could have done. Some further step I could have taken. Talking to her more at Jekyll's. Following her instead of trying to confront him. Finding her after my own mind split and I found out exactly what Hyde was, and forcing her to flee the very real danger she had faced all alone.

So many 'could have's,' all of them things I'd

failed to do.

I got up from the chair, letting the remnants of the parcel fall to the floor, and stumbled to the window. I needed air. I needed to breathe. I needed --

FREEDOM!

The thought ripped through me, making the division in my head all the more noticeable and frightening. No. No, not now. He was taking over. He was coming to the surface. He was --

"Holmes?" Erik said, grasping my shoulders.

I lashed out, yelling at him to let me go and whirling around as the demand tore from my throat. My right leg could not support me in so quick and violent a movement and I fell. As I crashed to the floor, striking my elbow and biting my tongue, I heard Erik shout, "He's transforming!"

*****

Holmes, or the alter ego of Holmes, clawed his way to his feet minutes later by way of the chair. He leaned over its back and stared at Watson and myself, an almost reptilian quality present in the way his neck was undulating.

"So," he rasped, "I'm free once again." He noticed the note on the floor and snaked around the chair to retrieve it. "Edward Hyde wishes my presence, does he? He shall have it, and he shall *regret* it."

I glanced over at Watson, only daring to take my eyes from *this* Holmes for a moment. Watson's face was pale, his body slack, his expression devastated. This was the moment he truly believed what we'd said was true; a second, potent, dangerous personality was fighting for supremacy within Sherlock Holmes. And right now, the second one had won another battle.

Watson backed away, terror in his eyes. I remained where I was, just watching the third man. I would not try to stop him this time; instead, I would allow him to leave, follow him, and let him lead us straight to Hyde.

He did push past me seconds later. His shoulder roughly contacted with mine as he staggered his way out the door, down the stairs, and into the foggy night.

Carefully counting to ten, I took a deep breath and went to go after him when Watson stepped forward and grabbed my arm.

"Wh-what was that?" he demanded. "Erik, that was *not* Holmes."

"I know. It was the 'Hyde' side of Holmes. That was the man who caused me to fall into unconsciousness. That is the man the serum released within him. That is the man Holmes has been fighting against becoming since that initial transformation."

"This is why you've been watching him so closely."

"Yes."

"I apologize for doubting either of you. What can we do now?"

"You stay here. As he is now, Holmes is a very dangerous, bloodthirsty man. Not only that, he is going to meet someone whom we know has murdered twice now in cold blood."

"You intend to go after him, though," he stated.

"I intend to retrieve Holmes once he's transformed

back," I corrected.

"What makes this any safer for you?"

I leveled my gaze on Watson, giving him my most intimidating glare. "I've been a madman as well, Watson. I know how those two think. Plus, I must get my lasso. I will not be so careless with it again."

Watson nodded. "Good luck, Erik."

"Thank you."

I stole out into the night after the transformed Holmes.

"You came, Holmes. I must say, I'm surprised," was the first thing I heard as I stealthily approached where 'Holmes' and Hyde were.

"I challenged you to overpower me if you dared. You merely picked a different time and location," was the guttural reply.

"It was necessary."

"Indeed? Because you wanted a fresh kill?"

Hyde gave a sinister grin beneath his dark, empty eyes. "I could have had you for my fresh kill. But you, you haven't bloodied your hands once. How do you expect to kill me?"

When I heard that, I was eerily reminded of the conversation Holmes and I had exchanged when I offered him a chance to best me at fencing. He'd asked if I honestly expected him to be able to kill me. I had accused him of arrogance, but he corrected my error. He knew if I won, I would have no qualms about killing; however, he did not have my former lack of such inhibition.

The two began a slow circling and once again, I thought of wolves about to pounce, declaring one as the dominant male and one as the solitary hunter, doomed never to belong.

I wondered if this version of Holmes would even want to hold himself back, or would he relish the idea of ridding the world of Edward Hyde, completely bypassing the fact that a good, but tortured, man was beneath the surface?

Swinging myself down from my hiding place, I decided I would not let Holmes find out. I would not let the real Holmes live with that guilt. He would not bloody his hands, not even on one so despicable as Hyde, while I watched.

Holmes's senses were just as keen in this form, I found out, for he said, "Ah. We have a third in our midst. I believe he wants to stop us from coming to blows."

Hyde waited until I was in plain sight of them both before saying, "When did I ever insinuate fisticuffs?" He pulled his coat back to reveal my lasso, frayed at one end, held at his waist.

"You bastard," I growled at him. Now, a third wolf had joined the confrontation. "Did you choke her with it as well?"

"The whore? I stabbed her. Then slit her throat," he reported calmly. "My other self had given her money. Told her to get away from here. To escape me. A chance for a 'new life,' he called it. She was going to take it. I couldn't have that."

My God . . . The disturbing thought that perhaps I wasn't as insane as I'd thought ran through my mind. I had killed, yes. More than once. But always with a reason, either out of self-defense, self-preservation, or because the 'victim' in question was going to harm someone else. Never was it so meaningless of an act as not wanting someone to escape me. I'd had the chance to kill for that, down in my lair. I could have killed Raoul and given Christine no choice but to remain with me. I would have made her be mine.

Except she would have hated me. And I would have killed myself before ever harming a hair on that mahogany head.

Obviously, Hyde was not a self-sacrificing sort.

'Holmes' didn't seem to care about the lasso. In fact, he said, "If you have that, what am I to use except bare fists? Of course, even without a weapon, I will more than be a match for you."

"Let us see," Hyde said menacingly.

Hyde moved toward 'Holmes,' but I stepped between them, dodging a left hook from 'Holmes,' and a kick from Hyde. The kick clipped 'Holmes's' left shin and made the punch miss, and I took the opportunity to grip the lasso and yank it away from Hyde.

"Ah, you want us on even footing, Masked One?"

"No . . ." I murmured. "If it was to be even footing, I would not be here. For I have no doubt I excel over you both." I tucked my lasso into my cloak and cracked my knuckles loudly. "If either of you tries to attack, I will intercept. And since I choose not to, I will not lose."

Hyde almost appeared to want to challenge me, see if I was bluffing. I was not. I could easily physically overcome them both. But Holmes, I would not attack. Hyde, on the other hand, I would gladly have fought. But with our eyes locked on one another's, Hyde must have seen something in my gaze, something he could not overcome, because he turned away first.

"Again, I say," he began, addressing 'Holmes' more than me, "we shall meet again. Next time, we won't be interrupted."

Hyde shuffled off into the night and 'Holmes' made as if to follow him. I held my arm up in front of him, dangling about two feet of the lasso from my outstretched hand. "Remain where you are unless you wish to be tied up."

He stared daggers at me, but stopped moving.

The unfortunate thing was I had no idea how to bring the real Holmes back. Or rather, how to help him surface again. So I did the only thing I could. I hit 'Holmes' just hard enough to render him unconscious, and carried him back to Baker Street.

I just had to hope that when he woke, he would be the Holmes with which we were familiar.

Chapter Twelve - The Way Back

When I woke sometime around five in the morning on October eighth, my bones ached, my right thigh throbbed, and my head felt split in two. Well, I realized, it was more than a mere feeling. My mentality *was* split in two.

The transformations . . . The word 'nightmare' comes to mind, but does not begin to do it justice. It felt as if my skin was melting, peeling, melding, and re-forging itself into something . . . familiar, yet new. Unspeakable pain wracked my body, giving me unforeseen physical hardships after I transformed back. I was very fortunate to have Erik here, what with his knowledge of herbs and such. Otherwise, I'm quite sure I would have been confined to a wheelchair for several days after each transformation. The pain my leg caused me was indeed that severe.

As I adjusted my position after waking, a jolt of pain shot up my leg and I ground my knuckles into my thigh in an attempt to massage some of the throbbing away. Watson was nowhere to be seen. He must have gone home to his wife. Or perhaps . . . perhaps my transformation had permanently frightened him away.

Erik was slumped on the floor near the window, head down, hands gripping his lasso. A pang of guilt hit me as I realized Hyde had only gotten hold of it because Erik dropped it for worry about me. Anger surged through me then as well, when I began recalling vague details about the previous night. I wasn't able to dwell on it long, though, because another pang of nearly unbearable agony blasted through me.

I tried not to cry out, but my vocal chords disagreed. Erik stirred, opened his eyes, and stared at me. "Another of my mixes?" he slurred.

"Please," I said through clenched teeth.

He rose tiredly, tucking the lasso into a fold in his cloak, and deposited a packet of the mixture into a cup. Quickly, he made tea, poured some of it over the mixture, and with remarkable dexterity and quickness, brought it to me while stirring the contents without spilling a drop. When he brought it to me, he knelt down beside me, and gently held the cup to my lips as he rested a steadying hand on my shoulder.

"Drink," he instructed. "You can hold it yourself when the pain has begun to subside."

I nodded, and sipped at the hot liquid, feeling it seem to spread through my veins as I swallowed.

Minutes later, as Erik promised, the pain lessened enough that I could sit up without much pain, my own fingers wrapped around the mug, providing my hands with much needed warmth.

"Something troubles you," Erik stated.

"*Some* thing? More like many," I said.

"Yes, but one thing above the others. And I sense it bothers you that this is the most prevalent thing on your mind. You feel it should be secondary to something else."

I stared at him, practically slack-jawed. "Now I understand why Watson is so amazed when I do that to him. It truly is as if I reach into another's mind and extract their thoughts before they say a word."

Erik chuckled. "So the tables have turned on the infallible Sherlock Holmes."

He said it lightly, but I felt my eyes, undoubtedly my entire face, darken. "I am not infallible."

"Ah! Thus comes to the forefront what you believe should have been there all along."

"Pray tell me what you believe these thoughts to be," I challenged.

"What was most considered until a moment ago was your own dilemma of how to bring your mind back to one, instead of two. That caused you a large sense of guilt because you believe you should be thinking of Lucy, of how you feel you should have been able to save her."

"How did you draw these conclusions?"

"Am I correct?"

I sighed. "Yes. How did you arrive at these conclusions?"

He smiled at me. "Elementary, my dear Holmes."

I grinned back. "I am aware, thanks to Watson's writings, that people have begun using that expression. However, while I may be mistaken, I don't recall ever actually uttering those words in front of him."

"Really? It is quite a catchy phrase, though. Perhaps it is, however mistakenly, something that you shall be known for in the future."

"I would rather be known for my solutions to cases than a 'catchy phrase' I never actually said." I looked at him. "You are avoiding my question."

"Simply because the answer takes any sense of mystique out of the conclusions."

I glared at him until he grinned again and relented. "You talk in your sleep."

"I do? Odd, when Watson resided here, he never mentioned me doing that." I thought for a moment. "Of course, I suppose it is very possible he never actually saw me sleep . . ."

"It's also possible that your mind was arguing. I didn't know how to attempt to bring your better self to the forefront, so I knocked you out, hoping *this* you would emerge. You have, but I believe your 'other' put up a fight about it."

"It wouldn't surprise me. Unfortunately, I remember nothing after you telling me to remain where I was unless I wished to be tied up."

"I could not risk you going after Hyde."

"I know. I understand." We were silent for a few moments before I slammed my fist on the arm of the couch.

"Holmes?"

"I should have *saved* her! *Damnation!* I knew what Hyde was. I knew *who* Hyde was! Instead of hiding behind my experiments and theories, my fears of what would happen to me, I should have done something."

"Holmes, how do you know you could have? Jekyll tried to and he failed."

"He only failed because Hyde knew of the actions he took! She would still live, had I gone to her."

"Holmes, her blood is not on your hands, it's--"

"It *is* on my hands!" I raised my hands in front of me, staring at both sets of digits with disgust. "These hands could have saved her. Instead, through their inaction, they helped doom her. And look."

"What?"

I held out my right hand. "The index and middle fingers. Her blood *is* on my hands."

"Holmes, listen to me." He got up and retrieved a

cloth with warm water on it from the washroom, then came over to me, taking my hand and bathing my fingers so that the visible stain of blood would disappear. "You did not kill Lucy. You didn't help Hyde. Believe the words of someone who has murdered before: you are not responsible."

I sighed, pulling my hand from his gentle grip and looking at my fingers again. No one else would be able to, because the blood was washed away, but my eyes would see the stain for a long time to come.

"It's not that I don't appreciate your efforts, Erik. I do. I simply need to come to acceptable terms with this on my own."

"I know," he said. "But just because a man needs to make a journey on his own doesn't mean others around him won't try and make it easier."

"Thank you. I suppose I'm truly beginning to understand what you meant by that never-ending uphill battle."

Erik merely nodded, as if the conversation had gone exactly the way he expected.

*****

I spent the next three weeks alternating between complete seclusion in Baker Street, or patrolling London to search for any sign of Hyde. The first was an attempt to bring the fractured pieces of my mind back into balance. I certainly couldn't eradicate one or the other, so a unity of mind was my only option. The latter because I was no closer to reconciling with myself over Lucy's murder, and the constant searching and consequently, constant leg pain, gave me some small measure of penance.

Some nights proved too much for my leg, however, and I would find myself collapsing on a bench, or clutching a lamppost to stay on my feet. Those were the times Erik would appear, seemingly from thin air, and assist me back to Baker Street. He never spoke; he had no need for words. He was there to help me when he could. Physically helping me was about all the assistance he could give at that time, because he seemed to intuitively know that this was what I needed to do. It was part of the war raging inside me.

When I worked inside, something about my demeanor kept Watson away and Erik silent, but close by. Something for which, much like the nights I would patrol, I was very thankful. There were times I would find myself staring off into space, my thumb gently caressing my index and middle fingers. When I would pull myself back to whatever task was before me, I would notice Erik watching me, his eyes unreadable behind his mask.

It was difficult to know if I was truly making any progress with the concoctions meant to bring my mind back into balance. I can only imagine what the pharmacist I sent Erik to thought. A masked man requesting various odd, rare, and dangerous chemicals. But I had no other choices. I was aware I had to replicate and then improve the formula Jekyll had started with. However, I was second guessing myself, and I knew it. Both sides of my mind were battling for ultimate control; I could not afford to lose and therefore, had to remain vigilante at all times, despite the exhaustion I felt. But the difficulty of that task was increased tenfold by the simple knowledge that I was unsure if all the thoughts in my head were even truly my own. What if they were *his?* One false step from him and the chemicals I was mixing could become fatal. Not to my physical body, but to what I had thought was the dominant portion of my mind.

"Erik," I said one day at the end of October, "I need your word on something."

"What is that, Holmes?" he asked.

I explained my fear to him of my alternate self interfering. I put down the vial I held and rested my hands on the chemistry table. "If that should come to pass, if I am eradicated and my more evil side emerges, I want you to promise you will kill me."

"What?" He gaped at me incredulously. "Holmes, I couldn't! Not unless there was no other choice! And even then . . ."

"If he interferes with the new serum I'm attempting, there won't *be* any other choice." I put my fingers to my temples. "Erik, I beg of you. If you must, then restrain me and try your own experiments. But if they fail, kill me."

I looked at him again, watching his eyes flicker with uncertainty. "Please, Erik."

He gave a mirthless laugh. "I was wrong in the opera house, you know."

I furrowed my eyebrows. I didn't follow his leap of logic.

"I believed I would have no problem dispatching you. I was gravely mistaken."

"Erik . . ."

"As long as I am permitted to do my own tests to attempt to bring you back."

"Yes."

"Then . . . you have my word."

I nodded and looked back at the beakers and vials in front of me. I paused, not sure what to add to the base next.

"Holmes, can I be of any assistance?"

I opened my mouth to say no, but at the last second, I stopped. Perhaps always being determined to work alone was Jekyll's main downfall. Perhaps, had he had someone to help him, Hyde would not have emerged. At least, not so violently. Perhaps with Erik's help, I could bring the beast inside me back where it belonged, instead of being destroyed by it.

"Please do, Erik. I'm grateful for your interpretation."

He came over and stood behind my chair, gazing at the myriad of liquids and powders of varying colors and consistencies in front of us. Occasionally, he asked the name of a chemical or what I'd mixed it with. Or what would happen if I mixed this with that, or that with those. I explained it all in detail, though it seemed Erik was only confirming his own knowledge. He allowed me to explain without interruption, and as my explanation was coming to a close, a light of understanding shone in his eyes.

"I must leave briefly, Holmes. I believe I have our solution. Give me no more than an hour. I shall be back, and if I'm correct, your mind will be one."

Before I could even part my lips to ask what conclusion he'd come to, he had slipped silently from the room.

*****

"Holmes?" Watson said hesitantly, standing somewhat fearfully in the doorway. Erik had been gone roughly twenty minutes and I'd once again been staring off into space, mindlessly rubbing my fingers.

"Watson, please, come in. You needn't lurk in the doorway. You know you're welcome here."

"Yes, thank you. I just -- well, I wanted to make sure you were undeniably yourself before . . ." he trailed off awkwardly, setting his bag down, removing his hat, and holding it with both hands in front of his chest.

"Before risking the wrath of my other, less socially acceptable, self?" I smiled. "You have avoided me for quite some time. Was seeing me that way such a frightful experience?"

Watson exhaled loudly and stepped over to perch on the edge of the couch. "I must say, Holmes, I have never had an encounter like that before in my life. When Erik first described you being someone else, I doubted him. But as I would trust you, I had faith in him. Seeing it . . . watching you transform . .. right before my eyes . . ."

"It's not an ordeal any of us wish to see again, I assure you," I said.

"Holmes, I must ask . . . why did you do it? Why did you inject yourself? Make yourself a victim?"

"I . . . needed to know. I was not going to get the answer from Jekyll, so while it was not a path I wanted to traverse, it would give me what I needed."

Watson, to my surprise, chuckled.

"You laugh?"

"Only because Stamford was right."

"Oh? About what?"

"When he told me that I was the second person in

one day to mention needing rooms to him, he told me a bit about you. One thing he said was that you dabbled with chemicals and some would see you as rather cold, the kind of chap who would inject someone with some alkaline or poison, not out of malice, but simply to see the effects. Then he said that you were just as likely to do that to yourself."

I gave a brief smile. "He was correct. If I had no willing subject, or felt my experiment was too dangerous to subject to someone else, I would administer whatever solution to myself. I consider myself fortunate right now. Erik is out procuring something in the hopes of cementing my mind back into one piece."

"Why, Holmes, that's . . . that's wonderful!"

"Indeed, it is. Now we just have to wait for his return."

His return came some thirty minutes later when he very nearly flew through the door holding a vial of blue-green liquid. He headed straight for my chemistry table, asked me to give him free reign, and once I moved, he began mixing drops of things into my base. He heated it on the Bunsen burner, and added a small pinch of three powders until the liquid became a murky yellow in color. Smiling, he set it aside and we waited a tense fifteen minutes while it cooled. Then he added several other pinches of powder, stirred, added his own vial of the blue-green liquid, and the mixture turned bright pink. Erik smiled, quickly pulled my notepad and a pen to himself, and wrote down everything he had done. Then, he noticed Watson.

"Watson, I'm glad you're here. Do you have your doctor's bag with you? And are there any unused syringes inside?"

"Yes and yes." He went to the door to retrieve the requested needle. "Erik, are you sure this . . . *thing* is actually a cure?"

Erik took the syringe from Watson and prepared it. "As Holmes was describing the chemicals and their reactions to me, I remembered a mason I spent time with while growing up. He taught me a number of things, including how to mix mortar. He was amazed by my ability to perfect the mixture each time I made it. But, as with all masons, his lungs began to suffer. I started making pain management medicines for him. Similar to the ones I've given you, Holmes." He glanced at me a moment, then back to Watson. "I digress. I've made a study of man's brain; not only the psychological elements of it, but the anatomy. I found that with the mason, if I gave him a chemical that would trick his brain into thinking another part of his body was in a mild amount of distress, his brain would focus on that body part, his lungs would calm, and he could more easily accept the drink to help coat his lungs and ease his cough. I merely related that to this situation."

I nodded, believing I understood what Erik meant, and dreading the possibilities if I was right. Watson, on the other hand, was lost.

"Erik, I'm aware, as I've mentioned before, that I don't have the keen powers of observation and deduction that you and Holmes possess, but you have managed to completely mystify me!"

"It's simple, Watson," I interjected. "If I understand his implication correctly, he wishes to inject a kind of poison in me. It will make my alter panic because he does not want to die. So, either he will take over completely, in which case arrangements have been made, or he will join back with me, my mind will become one again, and I will overcome the poison."

Erik nodded, happy I had understood. Watson simply looked horrified.

"Holmes, you can't seriously be considering letting yourself be poisoned?!"

"If there is no other way, yes, that's precisely what I'm considering."

"But . . ." He turned to Erik. "Realistically, what are the chances for success?"

"I don't know," Erik answered. "Jekyll and Holmes are the only two people in the world to have split their minds through chemical means. There is only one thing I can guarantee as an absolute. This will cure him -- " Watson looked hopeful -- "or it will kill him."

Despite Watson's attempts to protest further, Erik tapped several times on the syringe to assure there were no air bubbles and Watson got a small cloth that he splashed with alcohol so I could disinfect the area inside my left elbow. With a growing sense of trepidation, I held my arm out, trusting Erik to be correct, or for death to embrace me quickly. Either way, I would be freed of my Hell.

I felt the sharp sting of the needle as it penetrated my skin.

Holmes winced as Erik inserted the needle. Our masked friend then motioned for me to come over and hold Holmes's other arm. After Erik emptied the contents of the syringe into Holmes's vein, he put the needle down and grasped his arm. I wasn't sure what kind of reaction to expect, but I knew we were holding Holmes in preparation of having to pin him down.

I found myself thinking back over the course of this case. Had I known the opera house's mystery would lead to this, I'd have certainly kept the managers' letter from Holmes. I didn't begrudge Erik his involvement in this case; far from it. I would not have known how to help Holmes when he transformed. But then, had Holmes never received the letter from the Populaire, he would never have been made so intimately aware of Jekyll's doings.

But, one cannot change the past. Erik did have a very distinct edge over me when it came to actions of insanity. He did not fear them the way that I did.

When I was an army doctor in Afghanistan, before meeting Holmes, I saw my share of horror. Men with infections like a fungus, eating away at their limbs. Skin that had been burned to an unrecognizable crisp. Soldiers who woke in the dead of night, screaming because the horrors of their dreams were too vivid. And while I could deal with the medical aspects of war, I found I had little talent dealing with the psychological trauma of it all. It was actually a relief to be discharged after that Jezail bullet hit me. That's not to say that I didn't take pride in my work or that I didn't admire and respect the soldiers' sacrifices; I very much did, on both accounts. But war and its effects are not something from which one easily recovers.

My thoughts as we waited for a reaction from

Holmes went along this scattered path, with only a thin thread holding them together: dread. I dreaded what could happen, I dreaded what had happened, I dreaded what might have to happen.

And it was as I stood there, holding Holmes's arm, that something did happen.

Holmes's eyes opened impossibly wide and he looked first at Erik, then at me. Then he began thrashing wildly. Erik was able to hang on and partially pin down Holmes's left side, but I was unprepared for the sheer amount of strength he would unleash. I was flung away, hitting my shoulder and falling to my knees.

All I could do was helplessly watch as Erik and Holmes grappled. Finally, Erik was thrown off and Holmes struggled to his feet. I got up to attempt to grab him, but Erik got there more quickly. He produced his lasso, seemingly from thin air, and had it around Holmes, pinning his arms to his sides before I could take more than two steps.

"You won't win!" Holmes shouted, glowering at both of us. Erik forced him to sit back down in the chair and securely tied him in place.

"Then who will?" Erik challenged.

I caught a glimpse of both men's eyes. They had a mirrored expression of insanity and danger, but Holmes's also had . . . anger, yes, but . . . anger mixed with a touch of fear?

For the first time, I felt a true spark of hope. The alternate Holmes was afraid. But afraid of what? Of being eradicated, of ceasing to exist as his own separate mentality, or of dying?

"*ME!*" Holmes bellowed at Erik. "I know there is

poison coursing through these veins. Do you really think that I would ever let him go because of your threats?"

Erik leaned in close, only inches from Holmes's face. He murmured quietly, threateningly, "Yes. You will."

Holmes let out a blood-chilling laugh and attempted to bite Erik. Erik jerked away and backhanded Holmes.

"Erik!" I shouted, appalled. He didn't even glance at me as he stood up straight again.

"Fools!" Holmes shouted savagely. "He will never get away from --" His face suddenly contorted in pain and he gasped.

"Holmes!" I cried, wanting to rush to his aid. The doctor in me hated seeing anyone suffer, especially a close friend.

"No!" Erik held an arm out to stop me. "He must fight this battle alone."

"Indeed," Holmes said through clenched teeth. I could see his fingers on the arms of the chair were bloody from attempting to claw away at the wood. His eyes were pained, but clearer and it gave me hope that we were speaking to the Holmes with which I was familiar. "Alone . . ." he gasped out. Then, a spasm snaked through his body and the dead expression came back to his eyes. "Yes, you would lead me to the front lines and then push me into battle without so much as a final warning. Isn't that your game," he practically spit out the next words, "Monsieur Erik?"

Erik was unperturbed. He said calmly, "All that you are is the echo of a nightmare. You are nothing in the face of the true Sherlock Holmes."

"I'll be all that's *left* of Sherlock Holmes!" His face contorted in pain again and he let out a choked gasp.

Very softly, I heard Erik murmur, "We're close now. Do not speak. Merely watch."

A million thoughts flurried through my head when he said that. Reminders of old cases with Holmes, his showing me the difference between 'seeing' and 'observing,' him telling me how his experiments with blood types was progressing when we first met, all these and more traveled into my mind and made me wonder if those days were over. I was reminded of 'A Study in Scarlet.' The man with the pills. One poison, one harmless. I found myself wishing, as horrible as it was, that this was more similar to that: a quick kill or easy survival. Even if Holmes survived this, it was turning out to be anything but easy. But if he died . . .

What, I wondered, could the world possibly be like without the undeniable genius that was Sherlock Holmes?

I was startled out of my trance by an anguished scream from Holmes. I managed to keep still, but once again, every muscle in my body urged me to go forth, to uphold the Hippocratic oath and help him in some way.

I assume Erik read my body language and garnered the same meaning, because he caught my eye and forcefully shook his head.

Meekly, I took a step back, letting him know I would exercise self-control. When I looked back at Holmes, it seemed, from the expression on his face, that the battle within him was in full tilt. He strained against the ropes that held him, arching his back and flinging his head back. After another agonizing scream, he went limp, his head rolling forward and his chin resting at an angle on his chest.

Erik reached forward cautiously. "Holmes?" he murmured.

No response.

Erik bid me to come closer, on Holmes's other side. I did, and we both stood in front of him, waiting. After a few minutes, Erik loosened the lasso. When nothing happened, we waited several more minutes, and then Erik undid the lasso completely. Holmes slumped over to one side.

"And now we wait," Erik said, catching Holmes and holding him in place. "He's breathing. This has not killed him. When he wakes, we will see who has won the war."

I nodded and kept a close eye on both Holmes and the clock. Two hours passed before he stirred even slightly. I knelt next to Erik, who had kept hold of Holmes and hadn't moved more than an inch the entire time.

"Holmes?" he and I breathed.

Holmes groaned, moved his head slightly, and put a hand to his temple. Then he brought his face up and opened his eyes.

I stumbled away, landing on my backside, and gasped.

Chapter Thirteen - The Confrontation

Utterson was kind enough, thanks to Holmes's investigation, to offer us an invitation to Jekyll's wedding. Watson and I carefully devised a plan because, despite not hearing anything of Hyde since his last confrontation with 'Holmes,' I remained unconvinced that he was actually gone.

I got to the church early, taking a seat in the balcony. Once the other guests began to filter in about forty minutes later, I kept a careful eye out for Watson. He chose a pew closer to the back and glanced up at me. Our eyes met and we nodded to one another.

The wedding began not fifteen minutes later. Everyone took their positions and, as the traditional music began to play, Emma walked down the aisle on Utterson's arm. When they were in front of the priest, Utterson kissed her hand, then placed it in Jekyll's, and took his place as Jekyll's best man. Nothing out of the ordinary happened. Henry Jekyll appeared to be in complete control. Our plan would still commence, however.

When the priest said, "Let anyone who thinks these two should not be joined speak now, or forever hold their peace," I heard the faint creak of the church's door opening. As the priest opened his mouth to continue, I heard a loud voice say, "I wish to contest this union."

There were numerous gasps and everyone turned around to see who would dare stand in a house of God and interrupt a wedding. I smirked to myself, because I knew exactly who would dare it.

When Jekyll turned and saw who the voice

belonged to, his eyes narrowed. My hand involuntarily went to the Punjab lasso at my hip, but I forced myself to be still. This was still Jekyll, after all. An angry Jekyll, but then, we were disrupting his wedding day.

"On what grounds are you contesting this union, Detective?" Jekyll demanded.

Sherlock Holmes caned up the aisle. "I doubt that you would want me to say it aloud, Henry." He came right up to Jekyll and Emma and removed a vial I knew was labeled HJ-7 from his coat. He spoke quiet words I knew only Jekyll and Emma would hear and only Jekyll would understand.

The people in the church began to murmur curiously. I caught Watson's eye again and we exchanged a worried look. Suppose this didn't work? Suppose Jekyll -- alone -- had been able to do what Holmes and I had only accomplished together? We hadn't figured it as likely, but then, splitting one's mind through chemical means wasn't likely, either. The three of us had been counting on the emotional turmoil it would cause Jekyll if someone contested his marriage to be enough to turn him into Hyde. Or, as Holmes hypothesized, get him to begin showing signs of holding back a transformation, which any of the three of us -- Holmes, Watson, or myself -- would recognize so as to remove Jekyll from the scene.

Finally, Holmes stepped back from the couple, gave a slight bow, and went to the first pew, where the guests grudgingly made room for him. I heard Jekyll attempt to make a joke about Holmes's appearance, and then the priest pointedly asked if he may continue.

It happened as he got to the last lines after the rings were exchanged. Jekyll swayed slightly, regained his

167

footing, and swayed again. No one appeared to notice except Holmes, Watson, and me. But then Jekyll nearly fell into Utterson and I barely caught the words, "Help me out of here, John."

"Henry?" Utterson and Emma both echoed.

Jekyll looked at Emma, then around, and shook his head wildly. "No. No! Not now! Ah!" He grabbed his abdomen and doubled over, pain contorting his features. "John, get me out of here . . ."

Emma went to move closer, but Jekyll ordered her, through gritted teeth, to stay away.

"Henry . . ." Holmes said, already on his feet.

"Get me out of here," he repeated. Then he seemed to find a burst of strength, straightened, and attempted to run down the aisle to the door of the church.

"Henry!" Emma shouted.

"No! Not now, not like this! This will kill me! Dear God, please don't let her see me like this! Not on our wedding day!"

"Henry!" Emma shouted again as Jekyll tripped and fell, sprawling out on his stomach in the aisle.

A man I recognized as Simon Stride approached Jekyll and knelt down, reaching out to put a hand on his shoulder. I couldn't help wondering why Stride was there. Unless he was invited out of respect for the late Sir Danvers.

Before I could speculate further, I saw Jekyll's head move and before I could shout a warning -- before any of us could shout a warning -- Stride was grasped by the throat.

"Henry!" Utterson yelled sharply.

"There *is* no Henry," he said, getting to his feet and

turning around, squeezing the other man's throat so he gurgled grotesquely. "Only Edward *Hyde.*"

"No! Henry, let him go," Emma begged.

Stride managed to choke out, "You're a monster."

That, strangely, seemed to infuriate Hyde. *"I'm* the monster?" He laughed. A cold chilling laugh that I'm sure sent a shiver up and down the spines of all the ladies, and many men, present. "No, I think not, Stride. For at least my wickedness is out there for all to see. You, however, are truly the worst kind of monster. A hypocrite who pretends to be both worldly and good. Yet inside, you are ugly as sin!"

Distantly, I realized Holmes was carefully trying to approach Hyde; Watson was moving as well, to cut Hyde off from leaving the church. My hand tightened around my lasso again, but I knew this was Holmes's fight now. No longer were they two wolves. This time they were hunter and prey.

Hyde noticed the stealthy movement around him and focused his glare on Holmes. "Don't move."

Holmes stopped. Hyde stared at him thoughtfully. "I know you . . . Don't I?"

"In a manner of speaking," Holmes replied. "I'm sure you'll understand what I mean when I say I was not quite myself at the time."

"Ha! I knew you were the one to steal the formula, even before showing it to Jekyll today. Yet you blamed its disappearance on me. I should release this . . ." he looked at Stride disgustedly, " . . . and kill you instead."

Hyde's grip seemed to loosen around Stride's throat and everyone but Holmes and me got an expression of relief on their faces.

"But then, I'd rather kill you both," Hyde said a moment later, snapping Stride's neck impossibly quickly and letting his body fall to the ground.

Emma and several other ladies let out short screams. Utterson cried out, "Henry, what have you done?"

Hyde whirled on Utterson. "There *is* no Henry. Only Edward *Hyde!*" he repeated viciously.

"No! That can't be true," Emma cried, pushing her way past Holmes to stand before Hyde. Holmes tried to grab her arm, but she slipped past him too smoothly.

Hyde glanced at his hand and hers before grabbing her roughly. She let out a short cry that was cut off when Hyde sneered, "We appear to be married, my dear. Shall I carry you off to our bridal bed?"

"Hyde, stop!" Holmes shouted, moving several steps closer. "She's no part of this. Don't harm her!"

"Then don't come near me! Do *not* touch Edward Hyde, or before God, she *dies!*"

I watched Holmes, paralyzed by indecision for perhaps the first time in his life. There was no way to discreetly give or to surprise Hyde by injecting the perfected serum into his veins if Holmes couldn't come any nearer. We knew it would save him, but Holmes wouldn't risk another life, especially not that of another woman.

Surprisingly enough, Emma seemed to know what to do. The tension left her body as she said, "Henry . . . I know you can hear me. Please, let me go. I know you, and I know you do not want to hurt me. Please." She slowly turned so she was fully facing Hyde and put her hand on his cheek, caressing it as she looked into his eyes.

"Please. For us. For our love. Let me go."

Hyde blinked and I saw his hold on Emma loosen as he staggered back a step. Holmes reached forward and grabbed her arm, pulling her away and placing himself between her and Hyde. Hyde . . . or had Jekyll regained control?

"Henry?" Holmes said questioningly to the man who had fallen to his knees. "Is it you?"

"Yes. Dear God, what have I done?" Jekyll looked up. "Holmes . . . I have to be freed from this Hell."

"Henry, I have the perfected serum here. This can---"

"No! No more serums, no more chemicals." He looked past Holmes and focused on Utterson. "John, come here."

Utterson stepped forward cautiously. He stopped a foot or so closer to Jekyll than Holmes was.

"You promised. Do it now. I can't fight him much longer."

"Henry, I . . ."

"You promised!" Jekyll yelled.

Holmes looked from one man to the other. "Don't throw your life away like this, Henry," he said harshly. I suddenly realized that Jekyll had extracted the same promise from Utterson that Holmes had from me. Should he fail in his attempts, Utterson was to kill him. "What about everything you hoped to accomplish?"

Jekyll looked at Holmes, then gazed sadly around the church. I knew not only what Jekyll saw, but how he felt about the scene in front of him. Stride's body, Emma in tears, the guests cowering away, fearful of the man they had once so respected and admired. "Whatever I could have hoped to accomplish has vastly been outweighed by the horrors I *have* accomplished. I can't go on this way, Holmes. You don't have the blood on your hands that I do."

Then, before Holmes could protest, Jekyll stood, grabbed the sword at Utterson's hip, and ran it through himself. Again, several ladies let out screams, and Emma ran to Jekyll's side as he fell.

"Watson!" Holmes yelled.

Already moving, Watson was on Jekyll's other side in seconds, but the man was already losing too much blood. Almost before Watson could find and apply pressure to the point of entry, Jekyll had breathed his last. Holmes knelt to close the man's eyes and Emma bent down to kiss her fallen love's lips one last time. "Rest, my tortured love. No one can harm you now."

Holmes stood after Emma murmured her sentiment of love, and I saw a single tear escape, unchecked, down his cheek.

Epilogue

Erik, Watson, and I attended Jekyll's funeral several days after the wedding ceremony. Emma could hardly stand the grief of having lost not only her father, but her beloved, and broke down when the coffin was lowered into the earth. Utterson guided her away and I spoke with her when the crowd began to disperse.

"Miss Carew," I said, "if there is ever anything I may do for you, any assistance I can give, please, do not hesitate to ask."

"Why did he do it? Mr. Holmes, what was he trying to accomplish?" she asked, her voice thick with tears.

"Utterson gave me his journal, and other notes on the subject that were found in his laboratory. I'm still reading through them, but I believe the experiment was about, ultimately, the nature of the demons that possess a man's soul." I sighed. "Henry believed that we are all made up of two distinct entities, always fighting for supremacy within our psyche. He wanted to eradicate the malevolent force within man, and thus created the serum to separate the two."

"But if he succeeded in the separation, why didn't he succeed in the eradication?"

"First, because I believe he wasn't sure exactly how to proceed until after the separation occurred. Then, if someone was trying to rid the world of you, would you quietly accept it, or would you fight it?" I asked.

"So, the more evil side . . ."

"Was loathe to be destroyed, and fought against it,

eventually taking full control."

Emma was quiet for a long moment. "I understand. But . . ."

"There are so many questions left unanswered?" I completed.

"Yes. What did good and evil have to do with his institutionalized father, for instance? Henry often mentioned that his experiment was inspired by his father."

"As far as I can infer from the journals, he felt that his father had had a rare and unexpected reaction to that battle of supremacy. It seems Henry was under the impression that the elder Jekyll's good side was overtaken, but the evil side was too suppressed to be released. So, his father's gradual decline was his good half losing, and it eventually reached full catatonia when his evil side won but could not get out."

"So, all of this, it was outwardly to help mankind, but it began because Henry was obsessed with saving his father."

"I believe so."

She nodded. "I can accept that. Knowing how desperate he was to save the man who raised him . . . it makes things a bit easier to bear."

I garnered that she did not know Jekyll's alter had killed her own father. That was something I would not torture her by revealing.

"I'm terribly sorry for your loss. I wish I-- I had been able to get to Jekyll sooner. Perhaps if my deductions had been hastier . . ."

"Mr. Holmes, you mustn't blame yourself. Henry made his own choices, forged his own path. You cannot blame yourself any more than I should blame myself for not making him stop this experiment when I saw it was getting out of hand."

"Thank you, madam. That does help, in a small way."

She looked toward the grave. "I shall miss him. So very much."

"As will I," I agreed.

We parted company and I caught up to Erik, who told me Watson had already left with Utterson to go over some medical and legal technicalities. I asked if he minded coming with me on a short excursion.

When we reached our destination, paid the hansom cab driver, and exited, Erik looked at me. "Holmes, why have we come here?"

Instead of answering, I said, "When I spoke with Miss Carew, she said she would miss Jekyll. I responded in kind. Yet, I'm wrong. I never rightfully knew the man. I know nothing of his habits, his likes, his dislikes. I know that he was obsessive when it came to something he wanted to accomplish. I know he was compassionate, because who but a man filled with compassion would experiment on himself to save his father? I know that as time went on, he turned into a more and more desperate, broken man. But there is so much more to Henry Jekyll. I didn't know him. And now I never will. How can I possibly miss someone I never knew?"

Erik remained silent by my side.

"He and I spoke about my monograph, 'The Book of Life,' where I've said that through a single drop, one may infer the existence of the Nile, or of an ocean, even if they've never seen such a thing before. It may well be true for objects. But I had often related it to people as well. Gleaning things about them from something as simple as their clothing, or the way they wrote on a piece of paper. Arrogantly, I assumed I could tell nearly everything about them from that one small bit. After reading passages from Jekyll's journal, I'm coming to the harsh conclusion of how very wrong I was."

"Holmes, you aren't necessarily incorrect," Erik said. "In fact, I know you are less than fond of Watson's writing style, but if his stories are reported even halfway accurately, you do have an incredible talent for discovering a large amount of information about people based on very small sources. For instance, Watson's older brother's watch. Perhaps you didn't know what the man would prefer for breakfast, but you concluded solid facts about his personality."

"The same could be said for Jekyll. Obsession and compassion give me two very definite motivators. Yet the man is dead, and with him, two others. I failed to save him and I failed to save his victims. So where does this leave me?"

"Alive and having learned a valuable lesson for your next case."

"If there is even to be a next case."

"You are despairing your abilities of detection because of this outcome, unfavorable as it is?"

I sighed. "Perhaps. Look around, Erik. We're here because I've thought in great detail about your words on madness, as well as the painful necessity of facing the demons in my past. I'm afraid I can't delve back quite as far as you were asking about previously, but this location holds another demon I've yet to completely eradicate

176

within me." I gripped my cane tightly.

"Moriarty," Erik breathed.

"And his henchman," I confirmed. "I should have known enough about Moriarty to realize someone would be waiting in the wings. But when I figured out his scheme, when I knew beyond any doubt that *he* would be here that night, personally involved instead of hiding in the shadows, I was so consumed by the idea of apprehending him, I didn't take into account one very important factor. Moriarty never does anything alone. Had I not overlooked that vital fact, I would not have this cane right now. I wouldn't live in chronic pain. I would still be every inch the detective I was three years ago!"

"Holmes," Erik said sharply. "Listen to me. You're doubting yourself, and that's understandable. But never, *never* assume to be less than you are because of a physical impairment. Leave assumptions like that to ones who choose to remain ignorant and then are amazed at your feats. As I said at the start of this case, and I can hardly believe you're getting me to use this cliché twice . . . it *is* what's inside that counts. Behind the mask," he said, tracing his mask lightly with the fingers of his right hand, "or beneath the cane," he said, barely touching my right hand with his left fingertips.

A thin smile touched my lips. "I asked what was inside me that was truly worth anything. I must admit, I find myself wondering that again, but the reason is rather *frighteniwasng.*"

"Frightening?" Erik gave me a slightly alarmed look. "How so?"

"I wonder if the serum has actually been perfected. I've been feeling that push in my head the past few days."

"Push?"

"Yes . . . It's the best way I could describe the more evil side of myself wanting to emerge. There was a push in my mind. As if someone was shoving against a malleable material. Recently, I've felt a . . . I suppose 'push' would be too strong of a word. It's more of a nudge. But it is there. And it is worrisome."

"Indeed. Do you believe our serum wasn't perfected? Or that your alter ego had some hand in diluting it somehow?"

"I don't see how he could have. But perhaps the serum *was* tainted somehow."

"Holmes, we can work together to fix this."

I fell into silence, not knowing how to answer him. On one hand, of course I wanted to perfect the serum and know that my mind was back in one piece. On the other, perhaps it was our location, but I was once again overwhelmed by the thought that this was where my life had ended.

"What did you say?"

Facing him, I said, "I wasn't aware I'd spoken aloud."

"Yes. I believe you said something along the lines of your life ending. Please, tell me that I misunderstood."

"The words, no. The context, most likely."

"Holmes, explain," he requested, a slight tone of alarm in his voice.

"Perhaps we're not meant to perfect the serum. Perhaps my life truly was supposed to end the night I was shot. Perhaps I should never have asked Watson to save me."

"Holmes, not that I'm not grateful, but why *was*

Watson with you that night? When I stayed with you after the opera house case, you confided to me that you've had minor dealings with Moriarty before and purposely kept Watson in the dark. You didn't want him harmed. Why would you ask him to come with you that night?"

I considered for a long moment. "I suppose because I felt he was needed. Something in my gut told me to include him."

"Ah-ha. Is it possible something in you knew the night would go badly and that Watson may perhaps be a saving grace?"

I gave him a wry grin. "Is that optimism I hear in your tone?"

He smiled. "Yes, well, even I can't be a pessimist all the time. Your darker moods are melancholic enough for us both."

Laughing briefly, I nodded in agreement.

"Holmes, listen to me. We'll work together and perfect the serum if you're truly worried about your 'Hyde' persona emerging again. Since Watson is a medical man, he may have some helpful suggestions as well. Among the three of us, we'll figure out the correct formula. Your mind will stay unified."

"Thank you, Erik. That is reassuring." Looking out across the water, I said, "I'll have to go after him, you know."

"Moriarty? Of course. I would expect nothing less of you."

"The question is, will I have anyone by my side when I do?"

"Holmes . . ."

"Erik, you are an invaluable asset to me. I could

not have solved this case without you. No, I couldn't have *survived* this case without you. Please, reconsider my offer to become my partner."

Erik sighed. "Holmes, it's not a role I can see myself inhabiting. I know what you would have me say, but I'm sorry. I can't. I'll be here for you, for any assistance you may need, and I will keep my eyes open for cases, but that's all."

Closing my eyes, I nodded. That nudge was becoming a throbbing at my temples and behind my eyes. "Erik, would you assist me back to Baker Street? I believe we have formulas on which to experiment."

He gave me a worried glance as we went back to the main street and hailed a cab for our return. I hoped his worry was needless, but the pulsing I felt worried me more than I cared to admit.

Also from Kate Workman

"All in all, this is an interesting take on this pair of iconic characters which will appeal to the vast majority of fans of either of them".

The Bookbag

Also from MX Publishing

Close To Holmes

A Look at the Connections Between Historical London, Sherlock Holmes and Sir Arthur Conan Doyle.

Eliminate The Impossible

An Examination of the World of Sherlock Holmes on Page and Screen.

The Norwood Author

Arthur Conan Doyle and the Norwood Years (1891 - 1894) – Winner of the 2011 Howlett Literary Award (Sherlock Holmes book of the year)

www.mxpublishing.com

Also From MX Publishing

In Search of Dr Watson

Wonderful biography of Dr.Watson from expert Molly Carr – 2nd edition fully updated.

Arthur Conan Doyle, Sherlock Holmes and Devon

A Complete Tour Guide and Companion.

The Lost Stories of Sherlock Holmes

Eight more stories from the pen of John H Watson – compiled by Tony Reynolds.

www.mxpublishing.com

Also From MX Publishing

Watsons Afghan Adventure

Fascinating biography of Watson's
time in Afghanistan from US Army
veteran Kieran McMullen.

Shadowfall

Sherlock Holmes, ancient relics and
demons and mystic characters. A
supernatural Holmes pastiche.

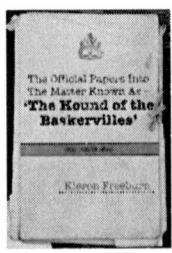

Official Papers of The Hound of
The Baskervilles

Very unusual collection of the
original police papers from The
Hound case.

www.mxpublishing.com

Also From MX Publishing

The Sign of Fear

The first adventure of the 'female Sherlock Holmes'. A delightful fun adventure with your favourite supporting Holmes characters.

A Study in Crimson

The second adventure of the 'female Sherlock Holmes' with a host of sub-plots and new characters joining Watson and Fanshaw

The Chronology of Arthur Conan Doyle

The definitive chronology used by historians and libraries worldwide.

www.mxpublishing.com

Also From MX Publishing

Aside Arthur Conan Doyle

A collection of twenty stories from ACD's close friend Bertram Fletcher Robinson.

Bertram Fletcher Robinson

The comprehensive biography of the assistant plot producer of The Hound of The Baskervilles

Wheels of Anarchy

Reprint and introduction to Max Pemberton's thriller from 100 years ago. One of the first spy thrillers of its kind.

Also From MX Publishing

Bobbles and Plum

Four playlets from PG Wodehouse
'lost' for over 100 years – found
and reprinted with an excellent
commentary

The World of Vanity Fair

A specialist full-colour reproduction
of key articles from Bertram Fletcher
Robinson containing of colour
caricatures from the early 1900s.

Tras Las He huellas de Arthur
Conan Doyle (in Spanish)

Un viaje ilustrado por Devon.

Also From MX Publishing

The Outstanding Mysteries of Sherlock Holmes

With thirteen Homes stories and illustrations Kelly re-creates the gas-lit, fog-enshrouded world of Victorian London

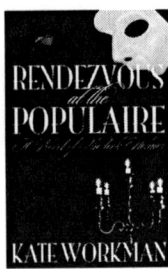

Rendezvous at The Populaire

Sherlock Holmes has retired, injured from an encounter with Moriarty. He's tempted out of retirement for an epic battle with the Phantom of the opera.

Baker Street Beat

An eclectic collection of articles, essays, radio plays and 'general scribblings' about Sherlock Holmes from Dr.Dan Andriacco.

www.mxpublishing.com

Also From MX Publishing

The Case of The Grave Accusation

The creator of Sherlock Holmes has been accused of murder. Only Holmes and Watson can stop the destruction of the Holmes legacy.

Barefoot on Baker Street

Epic novel of the life of a Victorian workhouse orphan featuring Sherlock Holmes and Moriarty.

Case of Witchcraft

A tale of witchcraft in the Northern Isles, in which long-concealed secrets are revealed -- including some that concern the Great Detective himself!

www.mxpublishing.com

Also From MX Publishing

The Affair In Transylvania

Holmes and Watson tackle Dracula in deepest Transylvania in this stunning adaptation by film director Gerry O'Hara

The London of Sherlock Holmes

400 locations including GPS co-ordinates that enable Google Street view of the locations around London in all the Homes stories

I Will Find The Answer

Sequel to Rendezvous At The Populaire, Holmes and Watson tackle Dr.Jekyll.

www.mxpublishing.com

Also From MX Publishing

The Case of The Russian Chessboard

Short novel covering the dark world of Russian espionage sees Holmes and Watson on the world stage facing dark and complex enemies.

An Entirely New Country

Covers Arthur Conan Doyle's years at Undershaw where he wrote Hound of The Baskervilles. Foreword by Mark Gatiss (BBC's Sherlock).

Shadowblood

Sequel to Shadowfall, Holmes and Watson tackle blood magic, the vilest form of sorcery.

www.mxpublishing.com

Also From MX Publishing

Sherlock Holmes and The Irish Rebels

It is early 1916 and the world is at war. Sherlock Holmes is well into his spy persona as Altamont.

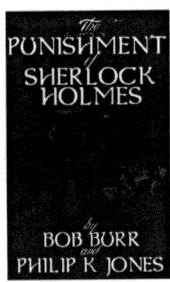

The Punishment of Sherlock Holmes

"deliberately and successfully funny"

The Sherlock Holmes Society of London

No Police Like Holmes

It's a Sherlock Holmes symposium, and murder is involved. The first case for Sebastian McCabe.

www.mxpublishing.com